The NONEXISTENT Knight
& The CLOVEN Viscount

BOOKS BY ITALO CALVINO

The Baron in the Trees
The Nonexistent Knight & The Cloven Viscount
Cosmicomics
t zero
The Watcher and Other Stories
Invisible Cities
The Castle of Crossed Destinies
Italian Folktales
If on a winter's night a traveler
Marcovaldo, or The seasons in the city
Difficult Loves
Mr. Palomar
The Uses of Literature
Six Memos for the Next Millennium
Under the Jaguar Sun

Italo Calvino

THE NONEXISTENT KNIGHT & THE CLOVEN VISCOUNT

Translated by Archibald Colquhoun

A Harvest Book
A Helen and Kurt Wolff Book
Harcourt Brace & Company
San Diego   New York   London

Harvest edition published by
arrangement with Giulio Einaudi Editore, S.p.A.

Library of Congress Cataloging-in-Publication Data
Calvino, Italo.
The nonexistent knight & The cloven viscount.
(A Harvest book)
Translation of Il cavaliere inesistente and
Il viconte dimezzato.
"A Helen and Kurt Wolff book."
I. Calvino, Italo. Il Visconte Dimezzato. English.
1977 II. Title: The nonexistent knight.
[PZ3.C13956N09] [PQ4809.A45]
853'.9'14   76-39699
ISBN 0-15-665975-1

Printed in the United States of America

I J K L M

CONTENTS

CONTENTS

The
NONEXISTENT
Knight

{ I }

BENEATH the red ramparts of Paris the army of
France lay marshaled. Charlemagne was due to review his paladins. They had already been waiting for
more than three hours. It was hot, an early summer
afternoon, misty, a bit cloudy. Inside their armor,
the men were steaming. Perhaps one or two in that
motionless row of knights went off in a daze or a
doze, but the armor kept them stiff in their saddles.
Suddenly there were three trumpet calls. Plumes on
charges swayed in the still air as if at a gust of
wind, and silence replaced a surflike sound which
must have come from the warriors snoring inside
the metal throats of their helmets. Finally, from the
end of the line, came Charlemagne, on a horse that
looked larger than life, beard resting on his chest,
and hands on the pommel of his saddle. With all
his warring and ruling, ruling and warring, he seemed
slightly aged since the last time those warriors had
seen him.

At every officer he stopped his horse and turned
to look him up and down. "And who are you, paladin
of France?"

"Solomon of Brittany, sire!" boomed the knight, raising his visor and showing a flushed face. Then he added a few practical details, such as, "Five thousand mounted knights, three thousand five hundred foot soldiers, a thousand eight hundred service troops, five years' campaigning."

"Up with the Bretons, paladin!" said Charlemagne, and toc-toc, toc-toc, he trotted on to another squadron commander

"Andwhoareyou, paladin of France?" he asked again..

"Oliver of Vienna, sire!" moved the lips as soon as the grill was up. Then, "Three thousand chosen knights, seven thousand troops, twenty siege machines. Conqueror of Proudarm the pagan, by the grace of God and for the glory of Charles King of the Franks."

"Well done, my fine Viennese," said Charlemagne. Then to the officers of his suite, "Rather thin, those horses, they need more fodder." And on he went. "Andwhoareyou, paladin of France?" he repeated, always in the same rhythm: "Tatatata-tatata-tata . . ."

"Bernard of Mompolier, sire! Winner of Brunamonte and Galiferno."

"Beautiful city, Mompolier! City of beautiful women!" And to his suite, "See he's put up in rank." All these remarks, said by the king, gave pleasure, but they had been the same for years.

"Andwhoareyou, with that coat of arms I know?"

He knew all armorial bearings on their shields without needing to be told, but it was usage for names to be proffered and faces shown. Otherwise, someone with better things to do than be reviewed might send his armor on parade with another inside.

"Alard of Dordogne, son of Duke Amone . . ."

"Good man, Alard, how's your dad?" And on he went. "Tatatata-tatata-tata . . ."

Godfrey of Mountjoy! Knights, eight thousand, not counting dead!"

Crests waved. "Hugh the Dane!" "Namo of Bavaria!" "Palmerin of England!"

Evening was coming on. In the wind and dusk faces could not be made out clearly. But by now every word, every gesture was foreseeable, as all else in that war which had lasted so many years, its every skirmish and duel conducted according to rules so that it was always known beforehand who would win or lose, be heroic or cowardly, be gutted or merely unhorsed and thumped. Each night by torchlight the blacksmiths hammered out the same dents on cuirasses.

"And you?" The king had reached a knight entirely in white armor; only a thin black line ran round the seems. The rest was light and gleaming, without a scratch, well finished at every joint, with a helmet surmounted by a plume of some oriental cock, changing with every color in the rainbow. On the shield a coat of arms was painted between two draped sides of a wide cloak, within which opened another cloak on a smaller shield, containing yet another even smaller coat of arms. In faint but clear outline were drawn a series of cloaks opening inside each other, with something in the center that could not be made out, so minutely was it drawn. "Well, you there, looking so clean . . . " said Charlemagne, who the longer war lasted had less respect for cleanliness among his paladins.

"I," came a metallic voice from inside the closed helmet, with a slight echo as if it were not a throat but the very armor itself vibrating, "am Agilulf Emo Bertrandin of the Guildivern and of the Others of Corbentraz and Sura, Knight of Selimpia Citeriore and Fez!"

"Aha . . . !" exclaimed Charlemagne, and from his lower lip, pushed forward, came a faint whistle, as if to say, "You don't expect me to remember all those names, do you?" Then he frowned at once. "And why don't you raise your visor and show your face?"

The knight made no gesture. His right hand, gloved in close-webbed chain mail, gripped the crupper more firmly, while a quiver seemed to shake the other arm holding the shield.

"I'm talking to you, paladin!" insisted Charlemagne. "Why don't you show your face to your king?"

A voice came clearly through the gorge piece. "Sire, because I do not exist!"

"This is too much!" exclaimed the emperor. "We've even got a knight who doesn't exist! Let's just have a look now."

Agilulf seemed to hesitate a moment, then raised his visor with a slow but firm hand. The helmet was empty. No one was inside the white armor with its iridescent crest.

"Well, well! Who'd have thought it!" exclaimed Charlemagne. "And how do you do your job, then, if you don't exist?"

"By will power," said Agilulf, "and faith in our holy cause!"

"Oh yes, yes, well said, that is how one does one's duty. Well, for someone who doesn't exist, you seem in fine form!"

Agilulf was last in the rank. The emperor had now passed everyone in review. He turned his horse and moved away toward the royal tents. He was old and tended to put complicated questions from his mind.

A bugle sounded "Fall out." Amid the usual confusion of horses, the forest of lances rippled into waves like a corn field moved by the passing wind. The knights dismounted, moved their legs, stretched, while squires led off their horses by bridles. Then the paladins drew apart from the rabble and dust, gathering in clumps of colored crests, and easing themselves after all those hours of forced immobility, jesting, boasting, gossiping of women and honor.

Agilulf moved a few steps to mingle in one of these groups, then without any particular reason moved on to another, but did not press inside, and no one took notice of him. He stood uncertainly behind this or that knight without taking part in their talk, then moved aside. Night was falling. The iridescent plumes on his crest now seemed all merged into a single indeterminate color, but the white armor stood out, isolated on the field. Agilulf, as if feeling suddenly

naked, made a gesture of crossing his arms and hugging his shoulders.

Then he shook himself and moved off with long
strides toward the stabling area. Once there he found
that the horses were not being groomed properly.
He shouted at grooms, meted out punishments to
stableboys, went his rounds of inspection, redistri-
buted duties, explaining in detail to each man what
he was to do and making him repeat the instructions
to see if they were properly understood. And as more
and more signs of negligence by his paladin brother
officers showed up, he called them over one by one,
dragging them from their sweet languid evening
chatter, pointing out discreetly but firmly when they
were at fault, making one go out on picket, one on
sentry duty or one on patrol. He was always right,
the paladins had to admit, but they did not hide their
discontent. Agilulf Emo Bertrandin of the Guildivern
and of the Others of Corbentraz and Sura, Knight
of Selimpia Citeriore and Fez was certainly a model
soldier, but disliked by all.

{ 2 }

NIGHT, for armies in the field, is as well ordered as
the starry sky: guard duty, sentry go, patrols. All the
rest—the constant confusion of an army in war, the
daily bustle in which the unexpected can suddenly
start up like a restive horse—was now quiet, for sleep
had conquered all the warriors and quadrupeds of the
Christian array, the latter standing in rows, at times
pawing a hoof or letting out a brief whinny or bray,
the former finally loosed from helmets and cuirasses,
snoring away, content at being distinct and differ-
entiated human beings once again.

On the other side, in the Infidels' camp, everything was the same: the same march of sentinels to
and fro, the guard commander watching a last grain
of sand pass through an hourglass before waking a
new turn, the duty officer writing to his wife in the
night watch. And both Christian and Infidel patrols
went out half a mile, nearly reached the wood, then
turned, each in opposite directions, without ever meeting, returning to camp to report all calm and going
to bed. Over both enemy camps stars and moon

flowed silently on. Nowhere is sleep so deep as in
the army.

Only Agilulf found no relief. In his white armor,
still clamped up, he tried to stretch out in his tent,
one of the most ordered and comfortable in the
Christian camp. He continued to think, not the lazy
meandering thoughts of one about to fall asleep, but
exact and definite thoughts. He raised himself on an
elbow, and felt the need to apply himself to some
manual job, like shining his sword, which was already
resplendent, or smearing the joints of his armor with
grease. This impulse did not last long. Soon he was
on his feet, moving out of the tent, taking up his
lance and shield, and his whitish shadow moved over
the camp. From cone-shaped tents rose a concert of
heavy breathing. What it was like to shut one's eyes,
lose consciousness, plunge into emptiness for a few
hours and then wake up and find oneself the same
as before, linked with the threads of one's life again,
Agilulf could not know, and his envy for the faculty
of sleep possessed by people who existed, was vague,
like something he could not even conceive of. What
bothered him more was the sight of bare feet sticking up here and there from under tents, with toes up-
turned. The camp in sleep was a realm of bodies, a
stretch of Adam's old flesh, reeking from the wine
and the sweat of the warriors' day, while on the
threshold of pavilions lay messy heaps of empty armor
which squires and retainers would shine and order in
the morning. Agilulf passed by, attentive, nervous and
proud; people's bodies gave him a disagreeable feeling

resembling envy, but also a stab of pride, of contemptuous superiority. Here were his famous colleagues, the glorious paladins, but what were they? Here was their armor, proof of rank and name, of feats of power and worth, all reduced to a shell, to empty iron, and there lay the men themselves, snoring away, faces thrust into pillows with a thread of spittle dribbling from open lips. But he could not be taken into pieces or dismembered; he was, and remained, every moment of the day and night, Agilulf Bertrandin of the Guildivern and of the Others of Corbentraz and Sura, armed Knight of Selimpia Citeriore and Fez, on such-and-such a day, having carried out such-and-such actions to the glory of the Christian arms, and assumed in the Emperor Charlemagne's army the command of such-and-such troops. He possessed the finest, whitest armor, inseparable from him, in the whole camp. He was a better officer than many who vaunted themselves illustrious, the best of all officers, in fact. Yet there he was, walking unhappily in the night.

He heard a voice. "Sir officer, excuse me, but when does the guard change? They've left me here for three hours already!" It was a sentry, leaning on a lance as if he had a stomach ache.

Agilulf did not even turn. He said, "You're mistaken, I'm not the guard officer," and passed on.

"I'm sorry, sir officer. Seeing you walking around here I thought . . ."

The slightest failure on duty gave Agilulf a mania to inspect everything and search out other errors and

negligences, a sharp reaction to things ill done, out
of place . . . But having no authority to carry out such
an inspection at that hour, even this attitude of his
could seem improper, ill disciplined. Agilulf tried
to control himself, to limit his interest to particular
matters which would fall to him the next day, such
as ordering arms' racks for pikes, or arranging for hay
to be kept dry. But his white shadow was continually
getting entangled with the guard commander, the
duty officer, a patrol wandering into a cellar looking
for a demijohn of wine from the night before. Every
time Agilulf had a moment's uncertainty whether to
behave like someone who could impose a respect
for authority by his presence alone, or like one who
is not where he is supposed to be, he would step back
discreetly, pretending not to be there at all. In his
uncertainty he stopped, thought, but did not succeed
in taking up either attitude. He just felt himself
a nuisance all round and longed for any contact with
his neighbor, even if it meant shouting orders or
curses, or grunting swear words like comrades in a
tavern. But instead he mumbled a few incomprehensible words of greeting, and moved on. Still hoping
they might say a word to him he would turn round
slightly with a "Yes?," then would realise at once
that no one was talking to him, and would run off, like
someone trying to escape.

He moved toward the edge of the camp, to a
solitary place. The calm night was ruffled only by a
soft flight of formless little shadows with silent wings,
moving around with no direction—bats. Even their

wretched bodies, half rat half bird, were something tangible and definite. They could flutter in the air, open-mouthed, swallowing mosquitoes, while Agilulf with all his armor was pierced through every chink by gusts of wind, flights of mosquitoes, and the rays of the moon. A vague anger that had been growing inside of him suddenly exploded. He drew his sword from his sheath, seized it in both hands and waved it wildly in the air against every low-flying bat. Nothing —they continued their flight without beginning or end, scarcely shaken by the movement of air. Agilulf swung blow after blow at them, now not even trying to hit the bats. His lunges followed more regular trajectories, and ordered themselves according to the rules of saber fencing. Now Agilulf was beginning to do his exercises, as if training for the next battle, testing the theory of parry, transverse, and feint.

Suddenly he stopped. A youth had appeared from behind a bush on the slope and was looking at him. He was only armed with a sword and had a light cuirass strapped to his chest.

"Oh, knight!" he exclaimed. "I didn't want to interrupt you! Are you exercising for the battle? There's to be a battle at dawn tomorrow, isn't there? May I exercise with you?" And after a silence, "I reached camp yesterday . . . It will be my first battle . . . It's all so different from what I expected . . ."

Agilulf was standing sideways, sword close to his chest, arms crossed, all behind his shield. "Arrangements for armed encounters decided by headquarters are communicated to officers and troops one hour before the start of operations," he said.

The youth looked a little dismayed, as if checked in his course, but overcoming a slight stutter, he went on with his former warmth. "Well, you see, I only just got here . . . to avenge my father . . . And I wish you experienced old soldiers would please tell me how I can get into battle right opposite that pagan dog Isohar and break my lance in his ribs, as he did to my heroic father, whom God will hold in glory forever, the late Marquis Gerard of Roussillon!"

"That's quite simple, my lad," said Agilulf, and there was a certain warmth in his voice, the warmth of one who knows rules and regulations by heart and enjoys showing his own competence, and confusing other's ignorance. "You must put in a request to the Superintendency of Duels, Feuds and Besmirched Honor, specifying the motives for your request, and it will then be considered how to best place you in a position to attain the satisfaction you desire."

The youth, expecting at least a sign of surprised reverence at the sound of his father's name, was mortified more by the tone than the sense of this speech. Then he tried to reflect on the words used by the knight, but so as not to admit their meaning, and also to keep up his enthusiasm, he said, "But sir knight, it's not the superintendents who're worrying me, please don't think that. What I'm asking myself is whether in actual battle the courage I feel now, the excitement which seems enough to gut not one but a hundred Infidels, and my skill in arms too, as I'm well trained, you know, I mean if in all that confusion before getting my bearings . . . Suppose I don't find that dog, suppose he escapes me? I'd like to know just what you do in such a case, sir knight, can you tell me that? When a personal matter is at stake in battle, a matter concerning yourself and yourself alone . . ."

Agilulf replied dryly, "I keep to the rules. Do that yourself and you won't make a mistake."

"Oh, I'm so sorry," exclaimed the youth, looking crestfallen. "I didn't want to be a nuisance. I really would have liked to try a little fencing exercise with you, with a paladin! I'm good at fencing, you know, but sometimes in the early morning my muscles feel slack and cold and don't respond as I'd like. D'you find that too?"

"No, I do not," said Agilulf, and turning his back, he walked away.

The youth wandered into the camp. It was the uncertain hour preceding dawn. Among the pavilions could be seen signs of early movement. Headquarters was already astir before the rising bugle. Torches were being lit in staff and orderly tents, contrasting with the half light filtering in from the sky. Was it really a day of battle, this one beginning, as the rumor went the night before? The new arrival was a prey to excitement, but a different excitement from what he had expected or felt till then. Rather, it was an anxiety to feel ground under his feet again, now that all he touched seemed to ring empty.

He met paladins already locked into their gleaming armor and plumed round helmets, their faces covered by visors. The youth turned round to look at them and longed to imitate their bearing, the proud way they swung on hips, breastplate, helmet and shoulder plates, as if made all in one piece! Here he was, among the invincible paladins. Here he was, ready to emulate them in battle, arms in hand, to become like them! But the two he was following, instead of mounting their horses, sat down behind a table covered with papers. They were obviously important commanders. The youth rushed forward to introduce himself. "I am Raimbaut of Roussillon, squire, son of the late Marquis Gerard! I've come to enroll so as to avenge my father who died an heroic death beneath the ramparts of Seville!"

The two raised their hands to their plumed helmets, lifted them by detaching headpiece and basinet, and put them on the table. From under the helmets appeared two bald yellowish heads, two faces with soft pouchy skin and straggly moustaches, the faces of clerks, of scribbling bureaucrats. "Roussillon, Roussillon," they mumbled, turning over rolls with saliva-damped thumbs. "But we've already matriculated you yesterday! What d'you want? Why aren't you with your unit?"

"Oh, I don't know, last night I couldn't sleep at the thought of battle. I must avenge my father you know, I must kill the Argalif Isohar and so find . . . Oh yes: the Superintendency of Duels, Feuds and Besmirched Honor. Where is that?"

"He's just arrived, this fellow, and he already knows everything! How d'you know of the Superintendency, may I ask?"

"I was told by that knight, I don't know his name, the one all in white armor . . ."

"Oh, not him again! If he doesn't stick his nose everywhere—that nose he hasn't got!"

"What? Hasn't got a nose?"

"Since he can't get the itch," said the other of the two from behind the table, "he finds nothing better to do than scratch the itches of others."

"Why can't he get the itch?"

"Where d'you think he could get the itch if he hasn't got a place to itch? That's a nonexistent knight, that is . . ."

"What do you mean, nonexistent? I saw him myself! There he was!"

"What did you see? Mere ironwork . . . He exists without existing, understand, recruit?"

Never could young Raimbaut have imagined appearances to be so deceptive. From the moment he reached the camp he had found everything quite different from what it seemed.

"So in Charlemagne's army one can be a knight with lots of names and titles and what's more a bold warrior and zealous officer, without needing to exist!"

"Take it easy! No one said that in Charlemagne's army one can etc., etc. All we said was in our regiment there is a knight who's so and so. That's all. What can or can't be as a matter of general practice is of no interest to us. D'you understand?"

Raimbaut moved off towards the pavilion of the Superintendency of Duels, Feuds and Besmirched Honor. Now he did not let casques and plumed helmets deceive him. He knew that the armor behind those tables merely hid dusty wrinkled little old men. He felt thankful there was *some*one inside.

"So you wish to avenge your father, the Marquis of Roussillon, by rank a general! Let's see, now! The best procedure to avenge a general is to kill off three majors. We can assign you three easy ones, then you're in the clear."

"I don't think I've explained things properly. It's Isohar the Argalif I've got to kill. He was the one who felled my glorious father!"

"Yes yes, we realise that, but to fell an Argalif is not so simple, believe me . . . What about four captains? We can guarantee you four Infidel captains in a morning. Four captains, you know, are equal to an army commander, and your father only commanded a brigade!"

"I'll search out Isohar and gut him! Him and him alone!"

"You'll end in the guardhouse, not in battle, you can be sure of that! Just think a little before speaking. If we make difficulties about Isohar, there are reasons. Suppose our emperor, for instance, is in the middle of negotiations with Isohar?"

But one of the officials whose head had been buried in papers till then now raised it jubilantly. "All solved! All solved! No need to do a thing! No point in a vendetta here! The other day Oliver thought two

of his uncles were killed in battle and avenged them!
But they'd stayed behind and got drunk under a
table! We have these two extra uncles' vendettas on
our hands, a terrible mess. Now it can all be settled.
We count an uncle's vendetta as half a father's. It's
as if we had a father's vendetta clear, already carried
out."

"Oh, dear father!" Raimbaut began to rave.

"What's the matter?"

Reveille had sounded. The camp, in first light,
swarmed with armed men. Raimbaut would have
liked to mingle with that jostling mob gradually taking shape as squadrons and companies, but the moving armor sounded to him like a vibrating swarm
of insects, buzzing like dry crackling husks. Many
warriors were shut in their helmets and breastplates
to the waist, and under their hip and kidney guards
appeared their legs, in breeks and stockings, because
they were waiting to put on thigh pieces and leg
pieces and knee pieces when they were in the saddle.
Under those steel crests their legs seemed thin as
crickets'." Their way of moving and speaking, their
round eyeless heads, arms folded, hugging forearms
and wrists, were also like those of crickets or ants. So
the whole bustling throng seemed like a senseless clus-
tering of insects. Amid them all, Raimbaut's eyes
searched for something: the white armor of Agilulf,
whom he was hoping to meet again, maybe because his
appearance could make the rest of the army seem
more concrete, or because the most solid presence he
had yet met was the nonexistent knight's.

He found him under a pine tree, sitting on the ground, arranging fallen pine cones in a regular design: an isosceles triangle. At that hour of dawn Agilulf always needed to apply himself to some precise exercise: counting objects, arranging them in geometric patterns, resolving problems of arithmetic. It was the hour in which objects lose the consistency of shadow that accompanies them during the night and gradually reacquire colors, but seem to cross meanwhile an uncertain limbo, faintly touched, just breathed on by light; the hour in which one is least certain of the world's existence. He, Agilulf, always needed to feel himself facing things as if they were a massive wall against which he could pit the tension of his will, for only in this way did he manage to keep a sure consciousness of himself. But if the world around was instead melting into the vague and ambiguous, he would feel himself drowning in that morbid half light, incapable of allowing any clear thought or decision to flower in that void. In such moments he felt sick, faint; sometimes only at the cost of extreme effort did he feel himself able to avoid melting away completely. It was then he began to count: trees, leaves, stones, lances, pine cones, anything in front of him. Or he put them in rows and arranged them in squares and pyramids. Applying himself to this exact occupation helped him to overcome his malaise, absorb his discontent and disquiet, reacquire his usual lucidity and composure.

This is how Raimbaut saw him, as with quick assured movements he arranged the pine cones in a triangle, then in squares on the sides of the triangle, and obstinately compared the pine cones on the shorter sides of the triangle with those of the square of the hypotenuse. Raimbaut realised that all this moved by ritual, convention, formulas, and beneath it there was . . . what? He felt a vague sense of discomfort come over him at knowing himself to be outside all these rules of a game. But then his wanting to avenge his father's death, his ardor to fight, to enroll himself among Charlemagne's warriors—wasn't that also a ritual to prevent plunging into the void, like this raising and setting of pine cones by Sir Agilulf? Oppressed by the turmoil of such unexpected questions, young Raimbaut flung himself on the ground and burst into tears.

He felt something on his head, a hand, an iron hand, but it felt very light. Agilulf was kneeling beside him. "What's the matter, boy? Why are you crying?"

States of confusion or despair or fury in other human beings immediately gave perfect calm and security to Agilulf. His immunity from the shocks and agonies to which people who exist are subject made him take on a superior and protective attitude.

"I'm sorry," exclaimed Raimbaut. "It's weariness maybe. I haven't managed to shut an eye all night, and now I'm bewildered. If I could only doze off a minute . . . But now it's day. And you, who have been awake too, how d'you do it?"

"I would feel bewildered if I dozed off for even a second," said Agilulf slowly. "In fact I'd never come round at all but would be lost forever. So I keep wide awake every second of the day and night."

"It must be awful . . ."

"No!" The voice was sharp and firm again.

"And don't you ever take off your armor?"

The murmuring began again. "For me there's no problem. Take off or put on has no meaning for me."

Raimbaut had raised his head and was looking into the cracks of the visor, as if searching in that darkness for the glimmer of a glance.

"How come?"

"How otherwise?"

The iron gauntlet of white armor had settled on the young man's hair again. Raimbaut hardly felt it weighing on his head. It was like an object that didn't communicate human warmth, proximity, consolation or annoyance—and yet, he felt a kind of tense obstinacy spreading over him.

{ 3 }

CHARLEMAGNE trotted along at the head of the
Frankish army. It was the approach march. There
was no hurry and they were not moving fast. Around
the emperor were grouped his paladins, reining im-
petuous mounts at the bit. In the trotting and jostling
their gleaming shields rose and fell like fishes' gills.
Behind them the army looked like a long gleaming
fish—an eel.

Peasants, shepherds and villagers gathered at the
corners of the road. "That's the king; that is our
Charles!" And they bowed to the ground at the
sight, not so much of his unfamiliar crown, as of his
beard. Then they straightened up at once to spot the
warriors. "That's Roland! No, that's Oliver!" They
never guessed right but it didn't really matter since
the paladins were all there, somewhere, so they could
always swear to have seen the one they wanted.

Agilulf trotted with the group, every now and
again spurting ahead, then halting and waiting for
the others, twisting round to check that the troops
were following in compact order, or turning toward

the sun as if calculating the time from its height above the horizon. He was impatient. He alone among them all had clearly in mind the order of march, halting places, and the staging post to be reached before nightfall. As for the other paladins, well, an approach march was all right by them. They were approaching anyway; fast or slow, it didn't matter to them. And with the excuse of the emperor's age and weariness they were ready to stop for a drink at every tavern. The road seemed lined with tavern signs and tavern maids. Apart from that, they might have been traveling sealed up in a truck.

Charlemagne was still more curious than anyone else about the things he saw around him. "Oh, ducks, ducks!" he exclaimed. A flock of them was moving through the fields beside the road. In the middle of the flock was a man, but no one could make out what the devil he was doing. He was walking in a crouch, hands behind his back, plopping up and down on flat feet like web-toes, with his neck out, repeating, "Quà . . . quà . . . quà . . ." The ducks were taking no notice of him, as if they considered him one of them. And to tell the truth there wasn't much of a difference between the man and the ducks, because the rags he wore, of earthen color (they seemed mostly bits of sacking) had big greenish-grey areas the same color as feathers, and in addition, there were patches and rents and marks of various colors like the iridescent streakings of those birds.

"Hey you, that's not the way to greet your emperor!" the paladins cried, always ready to make nuisances of themselves.

The man did not turn, but the ducks, annoyed by the voices, took alarm and all fluttered into flight together. The man waited a moment, watching them rise, beaks outstretched, then splayed out his arms and began skipping. Jumping and skipping and waving splayed arms, with little yelps of laughter and "Quà! . . . Quà . . . ," full of joy he tried to follow the flock.

There was a pond. The ducks flew onto the surface of the water and swam lightly off with closed wings. On reaching the pond the man flung himself on his belly into the water, raising huge splashes and thrashing his arms about. Then he tried another "Quà! Quà!" which ended in gurgles because he was sinking to the bottom. He reëmerged, tried to swim and sank again.

"Is that the duck keeper, that man?" the warriors asked a peasant girl wandering along holding a reed.

"No, I keep the ducks; they're mine. He has nothing to do with them. He's Gurduloo," said the little peasant girl.

"Then what was he doing with your ducks?"

"Oh nothing, every now and again he gets taken that way, and mistakes himself for one of them."

"Does he think he's a duck too?"

"He thinks the ducks are him. Gurduloo's like that, a bit careless . . ."

"Where's he gone to now, though?"

The paladins neared the pond. There was no sign of Gurduloo. The ducks, having crossed the piece of water, now began waddling along the grass on their webbed feet. Around the pool, from among the reeds, rose a croak of frogs. Suddenly the man pulled his head out of the water as if he had, at that moment, remembered he had to breathe. He looked around in a daze, not understanding this fringe of reeds reflected in the water a few inches from his nose. On each reed leaf was sitting a small smooth green creature, looking at him and calling as loud as it could, "Gra! Gra! Gra!"

"Gra! Gra! Gra!" Gurduloo replied, pleased; and at the sound of his voice frogs began to leap from every reed into the water, and from the water onto the bank. Gurduloo yelled, "Gra!" gave a leap out too and reached the bank, soaking wet, muddy from head to foot, crouching like a frog and yelling such a loud "Gra!" that with a crash of bamboo and reeds he fell back into the pond.

"Won't he drown?" the paladins asked a fisherman.

"Oh, sometimes Omoboo forgets himself, loses himself . . . No, not drown . . . The trouble is he's apt to end in our net with the fishes . . . One day it came over him when he'd started fishing. He flung the nets in the water, saw a fish just about to enter, and got so much into the part of the fish that he plunged into the water, and then into the net himself. You know what Omoboo's like . . ."

"Omoboo? Isn't his name Gurduloo?"

"Omoboo, we call him."

"But that girl there . . ."

"She doesn't come from our parts, maybe she calls him that."

"From what part is he?"

"Oh, he goes around . . ."

The cavalcade was now skirting an orchard of pear trees. The fruit was ripe. The warriors pierced the pears with their lances, making them vanish into the beaks of their helmets, then spitting out the cores. And there in the middle of a pear tree who should they see but Gurduloo—Omoboo! He was sitting with raised arms twisted about like branches, and in his hands and mouth and on his head and in the rents of his clothes were pears.

"Look, he's being a pear!" chortled Charlemagne.

"I'll give him a shake!" said Roland, and swung him a hit.

Gurduloo let all the pears fall down. They rolled down the slope, and on seeing them roll he could not prevent himself from rolling around and around, down the field like a pear. And so he vanished from sight.

"Forgive him, Majesty!" said an old gardener. "Martinzoo sometimes doesn't understand that his place is not amid trees or inanimate fruits, but among Your Majesty's devoted subjects!"

"What on earth got into this madman you call Martinzoo?" asked the emperor graciously. "He doesn't seem to me to know what's going through that pate of his."

"Who are we to understand, Majesty?" The old peasant was speaking with the modest wisdom of one

who had seen a good deal of life. "Maybe mad's not
quite the right word for him. He's just a person
who exists and doesn't realise he exists."

"That's a good one! We have a subject who exists
but doesn't realise he does and there's my paladin
who thinks he exists but actually doesn't. They'd make
a great pair, let me tell you!"

Charlemagne was tired now from the saddle.
Leaning on his grooms, panting into his beard, puffing,
"Poor France," he dismounted. As soon as the emperor set foot to the ground, the whole army stopped
and bivouacked. Cooking pots were put onto the fires.

"Bring me that Gurgur . . . What's his name?"
exclaimed the king.

"It varies according to the place he's in," said
the wise gardener, "and to the Christian or Infidel
armies he attaches himself to. He's Gurduroo or Gudi-
Ussuf or Ben-Va-Ussuf or Ben-Stanbul or Pestanzoo
or Bertinzoo or Martinbon or Omobon or Omobestia
or even the Wild Man of the Valley or Gian Paciasso
or Pier Paciugo. Maybe in out-of-the-way parts they
give him quite a different name from the others. I've
also noticed that his name changes from season to season everywhere. I'd say every name flows over him
without sticking. Whatever he's called it's the same to
him. Call him and he thinks you're calling a goat. Say
'cheese' or 'torrent' and he answers 'Here I am.' "

The paladins Sansonet and Dudon came up, dragging Gurduloo along as if he were a sack. They
yanked him to his feet before Charlemagne. "Bare
your head, beast! Don't you see you are before your
king?"

Gurduloo's face lit up. It was a broad and flushed face, mingling Frankish and Moorish characteristics: red freckles scattered on olive skin, liquid blue eyes veined with blood above a snub nose, thick lips, fairish curly hair and a shaggy speckled beard, the hair stuck all over with chestnut and corn husks.

He began doubling into bows and talking very quickly. The noblemen around, who had only heard him produce animal sounds till then, were astounded. He spoke very hurriedly, eating his words and getting all entangled, sometimes passing, it seemed, without interruption, from one dialect to another or even one language to another, Christian or Moorish. Amid incomprehensible words and mistakes, the meaning of what he said was more or less, "I touch my nose with the earth. I fall to my feet at your knees. I declare myself an august servant of your most humble majesty. Order and I will obey myself!" He brandished a spoon tied to his belt. "And when your majesty says, 'I order command and desire,' and do this with your scepter, as I do, with this, d'you see? And when you shout as I shout, 'I orderrr commanddd and desirrrre!' you subjects must all obey me or I'll have you strung up, you first there with that beard and silly old face."

"Shall I cut off his head at a stroke, sire?" asked Roland, unsheathing his sword.

"I implore grace for him, Majesty," said the gardener. "It's just one of his vagaries. When talking to the king he's confused and can't remember who is king, he or the person he's talking to."

From smoking vats came the smell of food.

"Give him a mess tin of soup!" said Charlemagne, with clemency.

Amidst grimaces, bows and incomprehensible speeches, Gurduloo retired under a tree to eat.

"What on earth's he doing now?"

He was thrusting his head into the mess tin which he had put on the ground, as if he were trying to get into it. The good gardener went to shake him by a shoulder. "When will you understand, Martinzoo, that it's you who must eat the soup, and not the soup you! Don't you remember? You must put it to your mouth with a spoon."

Gurduloo began lapping up spoonful after spoonful. So eagerly did he brandish the spoon that sometimes he missed his aim. In the tree under which he was sitting there was a cavity just by his head. Gurduloo now began to fling spoonfuls of soup into the hole in the tree.

"That's not your mouth! It's the tree's!"

From the beginning Agilulf had followed with attention, mingled with distress, the movements of the man's heavy, fleshly body, which seemed to wallow in existing, as naturally as a chick scratches. And he felt slightly faint.

"Agilulf!" exclaimed Charlemagne. "Know what? I assign you that man there as your squire! Eh? Isn't that a good idea?"

The paladins grinned ironically. But Agilulf, who took everything seriously (particularly any expression of the Imperial will), turned to his new squire in order to impart his first orders, only to find Gurduloo, after gulping down the soup, had fallen asleep in the shadow of that tree. He lay stretched out on the grass, snoring with an open mouth, his chest and belly rising and falling like a blacksmith's bellows. The dirty mess tin had rolled near one of his big bare feet. In the grass a hedgehog, attracted maybe by the smell, went up to the mess tin and began licking the last traces of soup. In doing this its prickles touched up against the bare sole of Gurduloo's foot, and the more it licked up the last trickles of soup the more its prickles pressed on the bare foot. Eventually the vagabond opened his eyes and rolled them around, without realising where that sensation of pain which had awoken him came from. He saw his bare foot standing upright in the grass like an Indian fig tree, and the prickle against his foot.

"Oh foot!" Gurduloo began to say. "Hey foot, I'm talking to you! What are you doing there like an idiot? Don't you see that creature is tickling you? Oh f-o-o-o-t! Oh fool! Why don't you pull yourself away? Don't you feel it hurting? Fool of a foot! You need do so little, you need only move a tiny inch! Look how you're letting yourself be massacred! Foot! Just listen! Can't you see you're being taken advantage of? Pull over there, foot! Watch carefully now. See what I'm doing; I'll show you . . ." So saying he bent his knee, pulled his foot toward him and moved it away from the hedgehog. "There, it was quite easy, as soon as I showed you what to do you did it by yourself. Silly foot, why did you stay there so long and get yourself pricked?"

He rubbed the aching part, jumped up, began whistling, broke into a run, flung himself into the bushes, let out a fart, another, then vanished.

Agilulf began moving to try and find him, but where had he gone? The valley was striped with thickly sown fields of oats, clumps of arbutus, privet, and swept by breezes laden with pollen and butterflies, and above, by clusters of white clouds. Gurduloo had vanished in it all, down that slope where the sun was drawing mobile patterns of shadow and light. He might be in any part of this or that slope.

From somewhere came a faint discordant song: *"De sur les ponts de Bayonne . . ."*

The white armor of tall Agilulf stood high on the edge of the valley, its arms crossed on its chest.

"Well, when does the new squire begin his duties?" asked his colleagues.

Mechanically, in a voice without intonation, came Agilulf's declaration. "A verbal statement by the emperor has the validity of an immediate decree."

"De sur les ponts de Bayonne . . ." came the voice still further away.

} 4 {

WORLD conditions were still confused in the era when this took place. It was not rare then to find names and thoughts and forms and institutions that corresponded to nothing in existence. But at the same time the world was polluted with objects and capacities and persons who lacked any name or distinguishing mark. It was a period when the will and determination to exist, to leave a trace, to rub up against all that existed, was not wholly used since there were many who did nothing about it—from poverty or ignorance or simply from finding things bearable as they were—and so a certain amount was lost into the void. Maybe too there came a point when this diluted will and consciousness of self was condensed, turned to sediment, as imperceptible watery particles condense into banks of clouds; and then maybe this sediment merged, by chance or instinct, with some name or family or military rank or duties or regulations, above all in an empty armor, for in times when armor was necessary even for a man who existed, how much more was it for one who didn't.

Thus it was that Agilulf of the Guildivern had begun to act and acquire glory for himself.

I who recount this tale am Sister Theodora, nun of the order of Saint Colomba. I am writing in a convent, from old unearthed papers or talk heard in our parlor, or a few rare accounts by people who were actually present. We nuns have few occasions to speak with soldiers, so what I don't know I try to imagine. How else could I do it? Not all of the story is clear to me yet. I must crave indulgence. We country girls, however noble, have always led retired lives in remote castles and convents. Apart from religious ceremonies, triduums, novenas, gardening, harvesting, vintaging, whippings, slavery, incest, fires, hangings, invasion, sacking, rape and pestilence, we have had no experience. What can a poor nun know of the world? So I proceed laboriously with this tale whose narration I have undertaken as a penance. God alone knows how I shall describe the battle, I who by God's grace have always been apart from such matters, except for half a dozen rustic skirmishes in the plain beneath our castle which we followed as children from the battlements amid caldrons of boiling pitch. (The unburied bodies that remained to rot afterwards in the fields we would come upon in our games next summer, beneath a cloud of hornets!) Of battles, as I say, I know nothing.

Nor did Raimbaut, though he had thought of little else in all his young life. This was his baptism of arms. He sat on horseback in line awaiting the signal for attack, but did not enjoy it. He was wearing too much. The coat of chain mail with its neckband, the cuirass with gorge guard and shoulder plates, the sparrow's beak helmet from which he could scarcely see out, a robe over the armor, a shield taller than himself, a lance which he banged on comrades' heads every time he swung it, and beneath, a horse he couldn't see, such were the caparisons of iron covering it.

The desire to avenge the killing of his father with the blood of the Argalif Isohar had almost left him. They had told him, looking at papers on which all the formations were set down, "When the trumpet sounds you gallop ahead in a straight line with set lance until you pierce him. Isohar always fights in that point of the line. If you keep straight you're bound to run into him, unless the whole enemy army folds up, which never happens at the first impact. Of course there can always be some little deviation, but if you don't pierce him your neighbor is sure to." If such was the case Raimbaut cared no more about it.

Coughing was the signal that the battle had started. In the distance he saw a cloud of yellow dust advancing, and another cloud rising from the ground as the Christian horses broke into a canter. Raimbaut began coughing. The whole Imperial army coughed and shook in its armor, quivering and shaking as it raced towards the Infidel dust, hearing more coughing getting nearer and nearer. The two dusts fused, and the whole plain rang with the echo of coughs and the clang of lances.

The aim of the first encounter was not so much

to pierce the enemy (as one risked breaking one's lance against his shield and what's more getting flung flat on one's face from the shock) as unhorse him by thrusting a lance between his saddle and arse at the moment of wheeling. This was a risky business, as a lance pointing downwards can easily get entangled in some obstacle or even stick in the ground and jerk a rider right out of the saddle like a catapult. So the first contact was full of warriors flying through the air gripping their lances. And side movement being difficult, since lances could not be waved far without getting into a friend's or enemy's ribs, there was soon such a bottleneck that it was difficult to understand a thing. Then up galloped the champions and began clearing a way through the mêlée.

Then they too found themselves facing the enemy champions, shield to shield. Duels started, but already the ground was so covered with carcasses and corpses that it was difficult to move, and when they could not reach each other they yelled insults. Here rank and intensity of insult was decisive, for according to whether offense given was mortal—to be wiped out in blood—medium or light, various reparations were laid down or even implacable hatreds transmitted to descendants. So the important thing then was to understand each other, not an easy thing between Moors and Christians and with the various Moorish and Christian languages; what did one do if along came an insult one just couldn't understand? One might find oneself swallowing it and being dishonored for life. So interpreters took part in this phase

of the battle, light-armed men swiftly mounted on fast
horses which swivelled around catching insults on the
wing and translating them there and then into the
language of destination.

"*Khar as-Sus!*"

"Worms' excrement!"

"*Mushrik! Sozo! Mozo! Enclavao! Marrano! Hijo
de puta! Zabalkan! Merde!*"

These interpreters, by tacit agreement on both
sides, were not to be killed. Anyway they galloped
swiftly away and if it wasn't easy in that confusion to
kill a heavy warrior mounted on a charger which could
scarcely move for its encrustation of armor, imagine
how difficult it was with these grasshoppers. But war
is war, as the saying goes, and every now and again one
did catch it. Anyway, even with the excuse of knowing how to say "Son of a whore" in a couple of
languages, they had to expect some risk. On a battlefield anyone with a quick hand can get good results,
particularly at the right moment, before the hordes
of infantry swarm over and mess up all they touch.

Infantry, being short little men, pick things up
best, but knights from up on their saddles are apt
to stun them with the flats of their swords and haul
up the best loot for themselves. "Loot" does not mean
things torn off the backs of the dead, as it takes
special concentration to strip a corpse, but all that
gets dropped. Since knights go into battle loaded with
supplementary harness, at the first clash a mess of
disparate objects falls to the ground. After that no
one can think of fighting, can he? The struggle now

is to gather everything up. In the evening on returning to camp the men bargain and traffic in the loot.
On the whole nearly always the same things pass
from camp to camp and regiment to regiment in the
same camp; what is war, after all, but this passing
of more and more dented objects from hand to hand?

Raimbaut found all that happened quite different
from what he had been told. On he rushed, lance forward, in tense expectation of the meeting between
the two ranks. Meet they did but all seemed calculated
for each knight to pass through the space between
two enemies without his even grazing another.

For a time the two ranks continued to rush on,
each in its own direction, each turning its back
to the other. Then they turned and tried to come to
grips, but by now impetus was lost. Who could ever
find the Argalif in the middle of all that? Raimbaut
found himself clashing shields with a man hard as
dried fish. Neither of the two seemed to have any
intention of giving way to the other. They pushed
against their shields, while the horses stuck their
hooves in the ground.

The Moor, who had a face pale as putty, spoke.

"Interpreter!" yelled Raimbaut. "What's he saying?"

Up trotted one of those lazybones. "He's saying
you must give way to him!"

"Oh, not by my throat."

The interpreter translated; the other replied.

"He says he's got to go on and get a certain job
done, or the battle won't work out according to
plan . . ."

"I'll let him pass if he tells me where I can find Isohar the Argalif!"

The Moor waved towards a hillock and shouted. The interpreter said, "Over there on that rise to the left!" Raimbaut turned and galloped off.

The Argalif, draped in green, was staring at the horizon.

"Interpreter!"

"Here I am."

"Tell him I'm son of the Marquis Roussillon, come to avenge my father."

The interpreter translated. The Argalif raised a hand with fingers clenched.

"Who's he?"

"Who's my father? That's your last insult!" Raimbaut bared his sword. The Argalif imitated him. He was a good swordsman. Raimbaut was already hard pressed when up came the Moor with the putty face, panting hard and shouting something.

"Stop, sir!" translated the interpreter hurriedly. "I'm so sorry, I got confused. The Argalif Isohar is on the hillock to the right! This is the Argalif Abdul!"

"Thank you! You're a man of honor!" said Raimbaut, then moved his horse, saluted the Argalif with his sword and galloped off toward the other slope.

At the news that Raimbaut was the son of the Marquis, the Argalif Isohar said, "What's that?" It had to be repeated more than once in his ear, very loud.

Eventually he yawned and raised his sword. Raimbaut rushed at him. And as their swords crossed doubt came over him as to whether this was Isohar

either, and his impetus was rather blunted. He tried
to work himself into a frenzy, but the more he hit
out the less he felt sure of his enemy's identity.

This uncertainty was nearly fatal. The Moor was
pressing closer and closer when a great row went up
nearby. A Moorish officer in the press of the battle
suddenly let out a cry.

At this shout Raimbaut's adversary raised his
visor as if asking for a truce, and called out in reply.

"What's he say?" Raimbaut asked the interpreter.

"He said, 'Yes, Argalif Isohar, I'll bring your
spectacles at once!' "

"So it's not him!"

"I am the Argalif Isohar's spectacle bearer," exclaimed his adversary. "Spectacles are instruments as
yet unknown to you Christians, and are lenses to correct the sight. Isohar, being short-sighted, is forced
to wear them in battle, but as they're glass a pair gets
broken at every fight. I'm attached to him to supply
new ones. May I therefore request that we interrupt
our duel, otherwise the Argalif, weak of sight as he
is, will get the worst of it."

"Ah, the spectacle bearer!" roared Raimbaut, not
knowing whether to gut him in a rage or rush at the
real Isohar. But what merit would there be in fighting a blind adversary?

"Do let me go, sir," went on the optician, "as
the plan of battle depends on his keeping in good
health, and if he doesn't see he's lost!" and brandishing the spectacles he shouted back, "Here Argalif,
here are the glasses!"

"No!" said Raimbaut, and slashed at the bits of glass, shattering them.

At the same instant, as if the sound of lenses in smithereens had been a sign of his end, Isohar was pierced by a Christian lance.

"Now," said the optician, "he doesn't need glasses to gaze at the houris in Paradise," and off he spurred.

The corpse of the Argalif, lurched over the saddle, remained hitched to the stirrups by the legs, and the horse dragged it up to Raimbaut's feet.

The emotion at seeing Isohar dead on the ground, contradictory thoughts assailing him—of triumph at being able finally to say his father's blood was avenged, of doubt whether *he* had actually killed the Argalif by fracturing his spectacles and so could consider the vendetta duly consummated, of confusion at finding himself suddenly deprived of the aim which had brought him so far—all lasted only a moment. Then he felt a wonderful sense of lightness at finding himself rid of that nagging thought in the middle of battle, and able to rush about, look round, fight, as if his feet had wings.

In his fixation about killing the Argalif he had paid no attention to the order of battle, and did not even think there was any. Everything seemed new to him, and exaltation and horror seemed to touch him only now. The earth already had its crop of dead. Fallen in their armor, they lay in awkward postures, according to how their greaves and joints or other iron accouterments had settled in a heap, sometimes with arms or legs in the air. At points the heavy armor had been breached, and from its interior stuffed guts spilled out of every gash. Such ghastly sights filled Raimbaut with horror. Had he perhaps forgotten that it was warm human blood that had moved and given vigor to all those wrappings? To all except one—or did the unseizable nature of the knight in white armor seem extended over the whole field of battle?

On he spurred, anxious to face living presences, friends or foes.

He found himself in a valley, deserted apart from the dead and flies buzzing over them. The battle had reached a moment of truce, or was raging on some quite other part of the field. Raimbaut was gazing around as he rode. There was a clatter of hooves; on the crest of a hill appeared a mounted warrior. A Moor! He looked around, reined in, then spurred his horse and galloped off. Raimbaut spurred too and followed. Now he was on the hills too. In the plain he saw the Moor galloping off and vanishing among the nut trees. Raimbaut's horse was like an arrow; it seemed to be longing for the chance of a race. The youth was pleased. Beneath those inanimate shells at last, a horse was a horse, a man a man. The Moor veered off to the right. Why? Now Raimbaut felt certain of catching up. But from the right now appeared another Moor, who jumped out of the undergrowth and barred his way. Then both infidels turned and came at him: an ambush! Raimbaut flung himself forward with raised sword and cried, "Cowards!"

One came at him, his black two-pronged helmet
like a hornet. The youth parried and banged the
other's shield, but his horse shied. Now the first Moor
began pressing him, and Raimbaut had to make play
with shield and sword and get his horse to twist round
in its tracks by pressing his knees to its sides. "Cowards!" he cried, and his rage was real, and his fight
was a real fight, and the effort to hold at bay two
enemies was agonizingly exhausting in bone and blood,
and maybe Raimbaut must die now that he is sure
the world exists, and does now know if dying is more
sad or less.

Both were on him now. He backed, seizing the
hilt of his sword as if stuck to it; if he lost it he was
done. At that extreme moment he heard a gallop. At
the sound, as at a roll of drums, both his enemies
broke away. They backed, protecting themselves with
raised shields. Raimbaut turned too; beside him he
saw a knight of the Christian armies with a robe of
periwinkle blue over his armor. A crest of long feathers
also periwinkle in color waved from his helmet. Swiftly
turning a light lance the warrior kept the Moors at
bay.

Now they were side by side, Raimbaut and the
unknown knight. The latter was still brandishing his
lance. Of the two enemies one tried to feint and
bounce the lance out of his hand, but the periwinkle
knight at that moment put his lance into its socket
on his saddle, bared his sword, and flung himself on
the Infidel. They duelled. Raimbaut, seeing how
lightly the unknown helper handled his sword, almost

forgot everything else to sit still and look. But it was only a moment; soon the other enemy launched himself with a great clash of shields.

So he went on fighting side by side with the periwinkle knight. Every time the enemy after a useless new assault found themselves backing, one took on the other's adversary with a rapid exchange, so confusing them with their different techniques. Fighting side by side with a companion is far nicer than fighting alone. Each encourages the other, and the feeling of having an enemy and that of having a friend fuse in similar warmth.

Raimbaut often shouted incitement to the other; but the warrior was silent. The young man realised that in battle one must save one's breath and was also silent, though rather sorry not to hear his comrade's voice.

The tussle grew fiercer. Then the periwinkle knight unhorsed his Moor; the latter escaped on foot into the undergrowth. The other rushed at Raimbaut but in the clash broke his sword; afraid of falling prisoner he too turned his horse and fled.

"Thanks, brother," exclaimed Raimbaut to his helper, opening his visor. "You've saved my life!" And he held out his hand. "My name is Raimbaut, son of the Marquis of Roussillon, squire."

The periwinkle knight did not reply, nor did he give his own name or shake Raimbaut's extended right hand or uncover his face. The youth flushed. "Why don't you answer me?" And at that moment what should the other do but turn his horse and gallop off! "Hey, knight, even if I do owe you my life, I consider this a mortal insult!" yelled Raimbaut, but the periwinkle knight was already far away.

Gratitude to his unknown helper, mute community born in battle, anger at that unexpected rebuff, curiosity at that mystery, excitement temporarily appeased by victory, and immediately on the lookout for other objectives—that was Raimbaut. He spurred his horse after the periwinkle warrior. "You'll pay for this insult, whoever you are!"

He spurred and spurred but his horse did not budge. He pulled its bit, and its snout dropped. He shook himself in the saddle. The horse gave a quiver as if made of wood. Then he dismounted, raised its iron mask and saw its white eye; it was dead. A blow from a Moor's sword had penetrated the chinks of the caparisons and pierced the heart. The animal would have crashed to the ground long before had not the iron pieces around his flank and legs kept it rigid, as if rooted to the spot. Sorrow for a valorous charger killed on its feet after serving him faithfully conquered Raimbaut's rage a moment. He threw his arms around the neck of the horse that was standing there like a statue, and kissed it on its cold snout. Then he shook himself, dried his tears and ran off on foot.

But where could he go? He found himself running over vaguely marked paths, beside a stream deep in woods, with no more sign of battle around him. All trace of the unknown warrior had vanished. Raimbaut meandered on, resigned now to losing him, but still thinking, "I'll find him again, though it's at the very end of the world!"

What tormented him most now, after that blazing

morning, was thirst. As he climbed down towards the surface of the stream to drink he heard branches moving. Tied to a nut tree by a loose bridle rein was a horse cropping at the grass, relieved of its biggest pieces of armor, which were lying nearby. There was no doubt; it was the horse of the unknown warrior, and the knight could not be very far away! Raimbaut flung himself among the reeds to find him.

He reached the river bank, put his head between the leaves; there was the warrior. Head and torso, like a crab's, were still enclosed in armor and in the impenetrable helmet, but the knee and hip pieces had been taken off, and the warrior was naked from the waist downwards and running barefoot over rocks in the stream.

Raimbaut could not believe his eyes. For the naked flesh was a woman's: a smooth gold-flecked belly, round rosy hips, long straight girl's legs. This half of a girl (the crab half now had an even more inhuman and expressionless aspect than ever) was turning round and looking for a suitable spot, set one foot on one side and one foot on the other side of a trickle of water, bent knees slightly, leant on the ground, arms covered with iron bands, pushed the head forward and the behind back and began quietly and proudly to pee. She was a woman of harmonious moons, tender plumage, and gentle waves. Raimbaut fell head over heels in love with her on the spot.

The young Amazon went down to the stream, lowered herself into the water again, made quick ablutions, shivering slightly, then ran up again with little

skips of her bare pink feet. It was then that she noticed
Raimbaut peering at her between the reeds. "*Schwein
Hund!*" she cried, pulled a dagger from her waist and
threw it at him, not with the gesture of a perfect man-
ager of weapons that she was, but with the impetus
of a furious woman throwing at a man's head a plate
or brush or whatever else she happens to have in her
hand.

Anyway she missed Raimbaut's forehead by a
hair's-breadth. The youth, ashamed, drew back. But a
moment later he longed to reappear before her and re-
veal his feelings to her in some way. He heard a
clatter and rushed to the field. The horse was no
longer there; she had vanished. The sun was declining;
only now did he realise that the entire day had gone
by.

Tired, on foot, too stunned by so many things
that had happened to feel happy, too happy to understand that he had exchanged his former preoccupation
for even more burning anxieties, he returned to the
camp.

"I've avenged my father, you know. I've won.
Isohar has fallen. I . . ." but he told his tale confusedly,
overhurriedly, since the point he wanted to reach
was another. "And I was fighting against two of them,
and a knight came to help me, and then I found out
it wasn't a soldier, it was a woman, lovely, the face
I don't know, in armor she wore a periwinkle blue
robe . . ."

"Ha, ha, ha," roared his companions in the tent,
intent on spreading grease on the bruises all over their

chests and arms, amid the great stink of sweat which is present every time armor comes off after battle. "So you want to go with Bradamante, do you, little one? If she wants! Bradamante only takes on generals or grooms! You won't get her, not even if you put salt on your tail!"

Raimbaut could not bring out a word. He left the tent; the sun was setting red. Only the day before, when seeing the sun go down, he had asked himself, "Where will I be at tomorrow's sunset? Will I have passed the test? Will I be confirmed as a man, making a mark in the world?" And now here he was at that next day's dusk, and the first tests were over. But now nothing counted any longer. There was a new test, and the new test was difficult, unexpected, and could be confirmed only there. In this state of uncertainty Raimbaut would have liked to confide in the knight with white armor, as the only one who might understand him; he had no idea why.

{ 5 }

BENEATH my cell is the convent kitchen. As I write I can hear the clatter of copper and earthenware as the sisters wash platters from our meager refectory. To me the abbess has assigned a different task, the writing of this tale. But all our labors in the convent have, as it were, one aim and purpose alone, the health of the soul. Yesterday, when I was writing of the battle, I seemed to hear in the sink's din the clash of lance against shield and armor plate, and the clang of heavy swords on helmets. From beyond the courtyard came the thudding of looms as nuns wove, and to me it seemed like the pounding of galloping horses' hooves. Thus, what reached my ears was transformed by my half-closed eyes into visions and by my silent lips into words and words and words, and on my pen rushed over the white sheet to catch up.

Today perhaps the air is hotter, the smell of cabbage stronger, my mind lazier, and the hubbub of nuns washing up can transport me no further than the field kitchens of the Frankish army. I see warriors in rows before steaming vats amid a constant clatter of

mess tins and tinkle of spoons, of ladles on edges of
mess tins, or scraping the bottom of empty encrusted
cooking pots; and this sight and smell of cabbage
is repeated in every regiment, from those of Normandy, Burgundy, and Anjou.

If an army's power is measured by the din it
makes, then the resounding array of the Franks can
best be known at mealtimes. The sound echoes over
valleys and plains, till eventually it joins and merges
with a similar echo, from Infidel pots. For the enemy
too are intent at the very same time on gulping foul
cabbage soup. Yesterday's battle never made so much
noise—nor such stink.

All I have to do next is imagine the heroes of my
tale at the kitchens. I see Agilulf appear amid the
smoke and bend over a vat, insensible to the smell
of cabbage, making suggestions to the cooks of the
regiment of Auvergne. Now up comes young Raimbaut, at a run.

"Knight," says he, panting, "at last I've found
you! Now I want to be a paladin too! During yesterday's battle I had my revenge ... in the mêlée ... then
I was all alone against two ... an ambush ... then
... now I know what fighting is, in fact. And I want
to be given the riskiest place in battle ... or to set
off on some adventure that will gain glory ... for
our holy faith ... to save women and sick and weak
and old ... you can tell me ..."

Agilulf, before turning round, stood there for a
moment with his back to him, in sign of annoyance
at being interrupted in the course of duty. Then,

when he did turn, he began to talk in rapid polished phrases which betrayed enjoyment at his masterly grasp of a subject put to him at a moment's notice, and of the competence of his exposé.

"From what you say, apprentice, you appear to believe that our rank as paladins consists exclusively of covering ourselves with glory, whether in battle at the head of troops, or in bold individual tasks, the latter either in defense of our holy faith or in assistance of women, aged and sick. Have I taken your meaning well?"

"Yes."

"Well, then, what you have suggested are in fact activities particularly recommended to our corps of chosen officers, but . . ." and here Agilulf gave a little laugh, the first Raimbaut had heard from the white helmet, a laugh courteous and ironic at the same time ". . . but those are not the sole ones. If you so desire, it would be easy for me to list one by one duties allotted to Simple Paladins, Paladins First Class, Paladins of the General Staff . . ."

Raimbaut interrupted him. "All I need is to follow you and take you as an example, knight."

"You prefer to set experience before doctrines then; that's admissible. Yet today you see me doing my turn of inspection as I do every Wednesday, on behalf of the Quartermaster's Department. As such I am about to inspect the kitchens of the regiments of Auvergne and Poitiers. If you follow me, you can gain some experience in this difficult branch of service."

This was not what Raimbaut had expected, and he felt rather put out. But not wanting to contradict himself he pretended to pay attention to what Agilulf did and said with cooks, vintners and scullions, still hoping that this was but a preparatory ritual before rushing into some dashing feat of arms.

Agilulf counted and recounted allocations of food, rations of soup, numbers of mess tins to be filled and contents of vats. "Even more difficult than commanding an army, you know," he explained to Raimbaut, "is calculating how many tins of soup one of these vats contains. It never works out in any regiment. Either there are rations which can't be traced or put on returns or—if allocations are reduced—there are not enough to go round and discontent flares up among the troops. Of course every military kitchen has hangers-on of different kinds, old women, cripples and so on, who come for what's left over. But that's all very irregular, of course. To clear things up, I have arranged for every regiment to make a return of its strength including even the names of such poor as usually line up for rations. We can then know exactly where every mess tin of soup goes. Now to get practice in your paladin's duties, you can go and make a tour of regimental kitchens, with the lists, and check that all is in order. Then you will report back to me."

What was Raimbaut to do? To refuse, demand glory or nothing? If he did he risked ruining his career over nonsense. He went.

He returned bored, no clearer than before. "Oh, yes, it seems to be all right," he said to Agilulf, "though it's certainly all very confused. And those poor folk who come for soup, are they all brothers by any chance?"

"Why brothers?"

"Oh, they're so alike . . . In fact they might be mistaken for each other. Every regiment has its own, just like those of the others. At first I thought it was the same man moving from kitchen to kitchen. But on the list there were different names: Boamoluz, Carotun, Balingaccio, Bertel. Then I asked the sergeants, and checked; yes, he always corresponded. Though surely that similarity . . ."

"I'll go and see for myself."

They moved towards the lines of Lorraine. "There, that man over there," and Raimbaut pointed as if someone was there. There was, in fact, but at first sight, what with green and yellow rags faded and patched all over, and a face covered with freckles and a ragged beard, the eye was apt to pass him over and confuse him with the color of earth and leaves.

"But that's Gurduloo!"

"Gurduloo? Yet another name! D'you know him?"

"He's a man without a name and with every possible name. Thank you, apprentice, not only have you laid bare an irregularity in our organization, but you have given me the chance of refinding the squire assigned to me by the emperor's order, and lost at once."

The Lorraine cooks, having finished distributing rations to the troops, now left the vat to Gurduloo. "Here, all this soup's for you!"

"All is soup!" exclaimed Gurduloo, bending over

the pot as if leaning over a window sill, and taking great sweeps with his spoon to bring off the most delicious part of the contents, the crust stuck to the sides.

"All is soup!" resounded his voice from inside the vat, which tipped over at his onslaught.

Gurduloo was now imprisoned in the overturned pot. His spoon could be heard banging like a cracked bell, and his voice moaning, "All is soup!" Then the vat moved like a tortoise, turned over again, and Gurduloo reappeared.

He had cabbage soup spattered, smeared, all over him from head to toe, and was stained with blacking. With liquid sticking up his eyes he felt blind and came on screeching, "All is soup!" with his hands forward as if swimming, seeing nothing but the soup covering eyes and face, "All is soup!" brandishing the spoon in one hand as if wanting to draw to himself spoonfuls of everything around, "All is soup!"

Raimbaut found this so disturbing that it made his head go round, not so much with disgust as doubt at the possibility of that man in front of him being right and the world being nothing but a vast shapeless mass of soup in which all things dissolved and tinged all else with itself. "Help! I don't want to become soup," he was about to shout, but Agilulf was standing impassively near him with arms crossed, as if quite remote and untouched by the squalid scene, and Raimbaut felt that he could never understand his own apprehension. The anguish which the sight of the warrior in white armor always made him feel was now counterbalanced by this new anguish caused by Gurduloo. This thought saved his balance and made him calm again.

"Why don't you make him realise that all *isn't* soup and put an end to this saraband of his?" he said to Agilulf, managing to speak in a tone without trace of annoyance.

"The only way to cope with him is to give him a clear-cut job to do," said Agilulf, and to Gurduloo, "You are my squire, by order of Charles King of the Franks and Holy Roman Emperor. From now on you must obey me in all things. And as I am charged by the Superintendency for Inhumation and Compassionate Duties to provide for the burial of those killed in yesterday's battle, I will provide you with stake and spade and we will proceed to the field to bury the baptized flesh of our brethren whom God now has in glory."

He also asked Raimbaut to follow him and so take note of this other delicate task of a paladin.

All three walked towards the field; Agilulf with his step which was intended to be loose but was actually like walking on nails, Raimbaut with eyes staring all round, impatient to see again the places he had passed the day before beneath a hail of darts and blows, Gurduloo, with spade and stake on his shoulder, not at all impressed by the solemnity of his duties, singing and whistling.

From a rise could be seen the plain where the cruelest fighting had taken place. The soil was covered with corpses. Vultures sat, with talons grappling the shoulders or the faces of the dead, and bent their beaks to peck gutted bellies.

The behavior of these vultures can scarcely be called appealing. Down they swoop as a battle nears its end, when the field is already strewn with dead lying about like Roman soldiers in steel breastplates, which the birds' beaks tap without even scratching. Scarcely has evening fallen when, silently, from opposite camps, crawling on all fours, come the corpse despoilers. The vultures rise and begin wheeling in the sky waiting for them to finish. First light glimmers on a battlefield whitish with naked corpses. Down the vultures come again and begin their great meal. But they have to hurry, as gravediggers are soon coming to deny the birds what they concede to the worms.

Agilulf and Raimbaut with blows of their swords, Gurduloo with his pole, thrashed off the black visitors and made them fly away. Then they set to their sorry task. Each of the three chose a corpse, took it by the feet and dragged it up the hill to a place suitable for scooping a grave.

As Agilulf dragged a corpse along he thought, "Oh corpse, you have what I never had or will have: a carcass. Or rather you *have*, you *are* this carcass, that which at times, in moments of despondency, I find myself envying in men who exist. Fine! I can truly call myself privileged, I who can live without it and do all; all, of course, which seems most important to me. Many things I manage to do better than those who exist, since I lack their usual defects of coarseness, carelessness, incoherence, smell. It's true that someone who exists always has a particular attitude of his own to things, which I never managed to have. But if their secret is merely here, in this bag of guts, then I can do without it. This valley of disintegrating naked corpses disgusts me no more than the flesh of living human beings."

As Gurduloo dragged a corpse along he thought, "Corpsey, your farts stink even more than mine. I don't know why everyone mourns you so. What's it you lack? Before you used to move, now your movement is passed on to the worms you nourish. Once you grew nails and hair, now you'll ooze slime which will make grass in the fields grow higher towards the sun. You will become grass, then milk for cows which will eat the grass, blood of the baby that drinks their milk, and so on. Don't you see you get more out of life than I do, corpsey?"

As Raimbaut dragged a dead man along he thought, "Oh corpse, I have come rushing here only to be dragged along by the heels like you. What is this frenzy that drives me, this mania for battle and for love, seen from the place where your staring eyes gaze, and your flung-back head that knocks over stones? I think of that, corpse; *you* make me think of that: but does anything change? Nothing. No other days exist but these of ours before the tomb, both for us the living and for you the dead. May it be granted me not to waste them, not to waste anything of what I am, of what I could be: to do deeds helpful to the Frankish cause; to embrace, to be embraced by proud Bradamante. I hope you spent your days no worse, oh corpse. Anyway to you the dice have already shown their numbers. For me they are still swirling in the box. And I love my own anxiety, corpse, not your peace."

Gurduloo, singing, began arranging to scoop out his corpse's grave. He stretched it on the ground to take its measurement, marked the edges with his spade, moved it, and began digging at full speed. "Corpsey, maybe you'll get bored waiting there." He turned it over on a side, towards the grave, so as to keep it in view as he dug. "Corpsey, you might help with a spadeful or two yourself." He straightened it up, tried to put in its hand a spade, which fell. "Enough. You're not capable. I see I'll have to dig it out myself, then you can fill the grave up."

The grave was dug, but so messy was Gurduloo's work that it turned out a strange irregular concave shape. Then Gurduloo decided to try it out. In he got and lay down. "Oh, how cosy it is, how comfy! What soft earth! How nice to turn over! Corpsey, do come and feel this lovely grave I've dug for you!" Then he thought a bit. "However, we've agreed that you must fill the grave, and it would be best if I stay down there, and you shovel the earth on me!" He waited a little, then, "Come on! Quick! It's nothing! This is the way!" And from where he was lying down in the grave he began shovelling earth down by raising his spade. And the whole heap of earth fell down on top of him.

Agilulf and Raimbaut heard a muffled cry, whether of alarm or satisfaction at finding himself so

well buried they did not know. They were just in time
to extract Gurduloo, all covered with earth, before he
died of suffocation.

The knight found Gurduloo's work ill done and
Raimbaut's insufficient. He himself had traced out
a whole little cemetery, marking the verges of rec-
tangular graves, parallel to the two sides of an alley.

On their return in the evening they passed a clearing in the woods where carpenters of the Frankish
army were cutting tree trunks for war machines and
fires.

"Now, Gurduloo, cut wood."

But Gurduloo swung blows in all directions with
his ax and put together kindling twigs and green
wood and saplings of maidenhair fern and shrub of
arbutus and bits of bark covered with mould.

The knight inspected the carpenters' ax work,
their tools and stacks, and explained to Raimbaut the
duties of a paladin for provisioning wood. Raimbaut
was not listening. All that time a question had been
burning in his throat, and now, when his outing with
Agilulf was near its end, he had not put it to him
yet. "Sir Agilulf!" he interrupted.

"What d'you want?" asked Agilulf, fingering an
ax.

The youth did not know where to begin, did not
know how to approach the only subject close to his
heart. So, blushing, he said, "D'you know Bradamante?"

At this name, Gurduloo, just coming up clutching
one of his composite bundles, gave a start. In the air

scattered a flight of twigs, honeysuckle tendrils, juniper bunches, privet branches.

Agilulf was holding a sharp two-edged ax. He brandished it, and buried it in the trunk of an oak tree. The ax passed right through the tree and cut it neatly, but the tree did not move from its trunk, so clean had been the blow.

"What's the matter, Sir Agilulf?" exclaimed Raimbaut with a start of alarm. "What's come over you?"

Agilulf with crossed arms was now examining all round the trunk. "D'you see?" he said to the young man. "A clean blow, without the slightest waver. Observe how straight the cut."

{ 6 }

THIS tale I have undertaken is even harder to write than I thought. Now it is my duty to describe that greatest of mortal follies, the passion of love, from which my vow, the cloister and my natural shyness have saved me till now. I do not say I have not heard it spoken of. In fact, here in the convent, so as to keep on guard against temptations, we sometimes discuss it as best we can with the vague notions we have about it, particularly whenever any of our poor inexperienced girls is made pregnant or raped by some powerful godless man and returns to tell us all that was done to her. So of love as of war I shall give a picture as best I can imagine it. The art of writing tales consists in an ability to draw the rest of life from the nothing one has understood of it, but life begins again at the end of the page when one realises that one knew nothing whatsoever.

Did Bradamante know more? In spite of that Amazon life of hers, a deep disquiet was growing within her. She had taken to the life of chivalry due to her love for all that was strict, exact, severe, conforming to moral rule and—in the management of arms and horses—to exact precision of movement. But what was around her now? Sweating louts who seemed to wage war in a very slack and slovenly manner, and who after duty were always mooning around her like boobies to see which of them she would decide to take back to her tent that night. For although knightly chivalry is a fine thing, knights themselves are crude, accustomed to doing great deeds in a slapdash way, only just keeping within the sancrosanct rules which they have sworn to follow and which, being so firmly fixed, take away any bother of thinking. War anyway is made up of a bit of slaughter and a bit of routine and doesn't bear being looked into too closely.

Bradamante was no different from them at heart; maybe she had got those ideas about severity and rigor into her head as contrast to her real nature. For instance, if ever there was a slattern in the whole army of France, it was she. To start with, her tent was the untidiest in the whole camp. While poor menfolk had to get down to work they considered womanish, such as washing clothes, mending, sweeping floors, tidying up, she, having been brought up a princess, refused to touch a thing. Had it not been for those old washerwomen and dish washers who always hang round troops—procuresses, the lot of them—her tent would have been worse than a kennel. Anyway, she was never in it. Her day began when she put on her armor and mounted her saddle. In fact, no sooner was she armed than she became another person, gleaming from the tip of her helmet to her greaves, each piece of armor more perfect than the last, with periwinkle tassels all over the robe covering her cuirass, each carefully in place. Her wish to be the most resplendent figure on the battlefield was an expression not so much of feminine vanity as of her constant challenge to the paladins, her superiority over them, her pride. In a warrior, friend or foe, she expected a perfection of turnout and weapon management as a reflection of similar perfection of soul. And if she happened to meet a champion who seemed to respond in some measure to her expectations, then there awoke in her the woman of strong amorous appetites. But there again, so it was said, she gave the lie to her own rigid ideals, for as a lover she was at one and the same time furious and tender. But if a man followed her in utter abandon, lost his self-control, she at once fell out of love or went searching for a temperament more adamantine. Whom could she now find, though? Not one of the Christian or enemy champions had ascendancy over her any more. She knew the weaknesses and fatuity of them all.

She was exercising at archery, in the space before her tent, when Raimbaut, who was wandering anxiously in search of her, saw her for the first time in the face. She was dressed in a short tunic; her bare arms were holding the bow, her face was a little strained with the effort; her hair was tied on the nape of her neck, then spread in a big fantail. But Raimbaut's look did not pause on details. He saw the woman as a whole, her person, her colors, and felt it could only be she, she whom, without having yet seen her, he desperately desired. For him, from now on, she could never be different.

The arrow winged from the bow, and pierced the target in an exact line with the other three which she had already put there. "I challenge you to an archery competition!" said Raimbaut, hurrying towards her.

Thus does a young man always hurry towards his woman. But is he truly urged by love for her, and not by love of himself? Isn't he looking for a certainty of existing that only a woman can give him? A young man hurries, falls in love, uncertain of himself, happy, desperate, and for him his woman is the person who certainly exists, of which only she can give the proof. But the woman too either exists or not. There she is before him, also trembling, and uncertain. How is it the young man does not understand that? What does it matter which of the two is strong and which weak? They are equals. But that the young man does not know, because he does not want to. What he yearns for is a woman who exists, a woman who is definite. She, on the other hand, knows more things, or less, anyway things that are different. What she is in search of is a different way of existing, and together they have a competition in archery. She shouts at him, does not appreciate him. He does not know that is part of her game. Around them are pavilions of the Frankish army, pennants in the wind, rows of horses eating fodder at last. Retainers prepare the paladins' meals. The latter, waiting for the dinner hour, are grouped around watching Bradamante at archery with the boy. Says Bradamante, "You hit the target all right but it's always by chance!"

"By chance? But I don't put an arrow wrong!"

"If you didn't put a hundred arrows wrong it would still be by chance!"

"What isn't by chance then? Who can do anything but by chance?"

On the edge of the field Agilulf was slowly passing. On his white armor hung a long black mantle. He was walking along like one who wants to avoid looking but knows he is being looked at himself, and thinks he should show that he does not care, while on the other hand he does, though in a different way than others may think.

"Sir knight, come and show him how . . ." Bradamante's voice had lost its usual contemptuous tone and her bearing its arrogance. She took two paces towards Agilulf and offered him the bow with an arrow already set in it.

Slowly Agilulf came closer, took the bow, drew back his cloak, put one foot behind the other and moved arms and bow forward. His movements were not those of muscles and nerves concentrating on a good aim. He was ordering his forces by will power, setting the tip of the arrow at the invisible line of the target; he moved the bow very slightly and no more, and let fly. The arrow was bound to hit the target. Bradamante cried, "A fine shot!"

Agilulf did not care, he held tight in his iron fist the still quivering bow. Then he let it fall and gathered his mantle around him, holding it close in both fists against his breastplate; and so he moved off. He had nothing to say and had said nothing.

Bradamante set her bow again, raised it with taut arms, shook the ends of her hair on her shoulders. "Who or who else could shoot such a neat bow? Whoever else could be so exact and perfect as he in his every act?" So saying she kicked away the grassy tufts and broke her arrows against palisades. Agilulf was already far off and did not turn. His iridescent crest was bent forward as if he were walking bent with arms tight across his steel chest, his black cloak dragging.

Of the warriors gathered around one or two sat on the grass to enjoy the scene of Bradamante's frenzy. "Since she's fallen in love with Agilulf like this the poor girl hasn't had a moment's peace . . ."

"What? What's that you say?" Raimbaut had caught the phrase, and gripped the arm of the man who had spoken.

"Hey you, little chick, puff your chest out for our little paladiness if you like! Now she only likes armor that's clean inside and out! Don't you know she is head over heels in love with Agilulf?"

"But how can that be . . . Agilulf . . . Bradamante . . . How?"

"How? Well, if a girl has had enough of every man who exists, her only remaining desire could be for a man who doesn't exist at all . . ."

Raimbaut found it was becoming a kind of natural instinct, in every moment of doubt and discouragement, to feel he wanted to consult the knight in the white armor. He felt this now, but did not know if he was to ask his advice again or face him as a rival.

"Hey, blondie, isn't he a bit of a lightweight for bed?" her fellow warriors called. Now Bradamante must be in a real decline. As if once upon a time anyone would have dared talk to her in that tone!

"Say," insisted the cheeky voices, "suppose you strip him, what d'you get?" and they roared with laughter.

Raimbaut felt a double anguish at hearing Bradamante and the knight spoken of so and rage at realising that he did not come into the discussion at all and that no one considered him in the least connected with it.

Bradamante had now armed herself with a whip and was swirling it in the air to disperse bystanders, Raimbaut among them. "Don't you think I'm woman enough to make any man do whatever I want him to?"

Off they ran shouting, "Uh! Uh! If you'd like us to lend him a bit of something, Bradamà, don't hesitate to ask!"

Raimbaut, urged on by the others, followed the group of jeering warriors until they dispersed. Now he had no desire to return to Bradamante. Even Agilulf's company would have made him ill at ease. By chance he found himself walking beside another youth called Torrismund, younger son of the Duke of Cornwall, who was slouching along, staring glumly at the ground and whistling. Raimbaut walked on with this youth, who was almost unknown to him, and feeling a need to express himself began talking. "I'm new here. I don't know, it's not like I thought, I can't catch it, one never seems to get anywhere, it all seems quite incomprehensible."

Torrismund did not raise his eyes, just interrupted his glum whistling for a moment and said, "It's all quite foul."

"Well, you know," answered Raimbaut, "I wouldn't be so pessimistic, there are moments when I feel full of enthusiasm, even of admiration, as if I understand everything at last, and eventually I say to myself, if I've now found the right viewpoint from which to see things, if war in the Frankish army is all like this, then this is really what I dreamt of. But one can never be quite sure of things . . ."

"What d'you expect to be sure of?" interrupted Torrismund. "Insignia, ranks, titles . . . All mere show. Those paladins' shields with armorial bearings and mottoes are not made of iron; they're just paper, you can put your finger through them."

They had reached a well. On the stone verge frogs were leaping and croaking. Torrismund turned towards the camp and pointed at the high pennants above the palisades with a gesture as if wanting to blot it all out.

"But the Imperial army," objected Raimbaut, his outburst of bitterness suffocated by the other's frenzy of negation, and trying not to lose his sense of proportion and to find a place again for his own sorrows, "the Imperial army, one must admit, is still fighting for a holy cause and defending Christianity against the Infidel."

"There's no defense or offense about it, or sense in anything at all," said Torrismund. "The war will last for centuries, and nobody will win or lose; we'll all sit here face to face forever. Without one or the other there'd be nothing, and yet both we and they have forgotten by now why we're fighting . . . D'you hear those frogs? What we are all doing has as much sense and order as their croaks, their leaps from water to bank and from bank to water . . ."

"To me it's not like that," said Raimbaut, "to me, in fact, everything is too pigeonholed, too regulated . . . I see the virtue and value, but it's all so cold . . . But a knight who doesn't exist, that does rather frighten me, I must confess . . . Yet I admire him, he's so perfect in all he does, he makes one more confident than if he did exist, and almost"—he blushed—"I can sympathise with Bradamante . . . Agilulf is surely the best knight in our army . . ."

"Puah!"

"What d'you mean, puah!"

"He's a made-up job, worse than the others!"

"What d'you mean, a made-up job? All he does he takes seriously."

"Nonsense! All tales . . . Neither he exists nor the things he does nor what he says, nothing, nothing at all . . ."

"How, then, with the disadvantage he is at compared to others, can he do in the army the job he does? By his name alone?"

Torrismund stood a moment in silence, then said slowly, "Here the names are false too. If I could I'd blow the lot up. There wouldn't even be earth on which to rest the feet."

"Is there nothing salvageable, then?"

"Maybe. But not here."

"Who? Where?"

"The knights of the Holy Grail."

"And where are they?"

"In the forests of Scotland."

"Have you seen them?"

"No!"

"Then how d'you know about them?"

"I know."

They were silent. Only the croak of frogs could be heard. Raimbaut began to feel a fear coming over him that this croaking might drown everything else, drown him too in a green slimy blind pulsation of gills. But he remembered Bradamante, how she had appeared in battle with raised sword, and all his unease was forgotten. He longed for a time to fight and do prodigious deeds before her emerald eyes.

{ 7 }

EACH nun is given her own penance here in the convent, her own way of gaining eternal salvation. Mine is this of writing tales. And a hard penance it is. Outside is high summer; from the valley rises a murmur of voices and a movement of water. My cell is high up and through its slit of a window I can see a bend of the river with naked peasant youths bathing, and further on, beyond a clump of willows, girls too have taken off their dresses and are going down to bathe. Now one of the youths has swum underwater and surfaced to look at them and they are pointing at him with cries. I might be there too, in gay company, with young folk of my own station, and servants and retainers. But our holy vocation leads us to esteem the permanent above the fleeting joys of the world. Which remains . . . and if this book, and all our acts of piety carried out with ashen hearts, are not already ashes too . . . even more ashes than the sensual frolics down at the river which tremble with life and propagate like circles in water . . .

One starts off writing with a certain zest, but a

time comes when the pen merely grates in dusty ink, and not a drop of life flows, and life is all outside, outside the window, outside oneself, and it seems that never more can one escape into a page one is writing, open out another world, leap the gap. Maybe it's better so. Maybe the time when one wrote with delight was neither a miracle nor grace but a sin, of idolatry, of pride. Am I rid of such now? No, writing has not changed me for the better at all. I have merely used up part of my restless, conscienceless youth. What value to me will these discontented pages be? The book, the vow, are worth no more than one is worth oneself. One can never be sure of saving one's soul by writing. One may go on writing with a soul already lost.

Then do you think I ought to go to the Mother Abbess and beg her to change my task, send me to draw water from the well, thread flax, shell chickpeas? There'd be no point in that. I'll go on with my scribe's duties as best I can. My next job is to describe the paladins' banquet.

Against all Imperial rules of etiquette, Charlemagne settled at table before the proper time, when no one else had reached the board. Down he sat and began to pick at bread or cheese or olives or peppers, everything on the tables in fact. Not only that, but he also used his hands. Absolute power often slackens all controls, generates arbitrary actions, even in the most temperate of sovereigns.

One by one the paladins arrived in their grand gala robes which, between lace and brocade, still showed chain mail cuirasses, the kind with a very wide mesh, worn with dress armor, gleaming like a mirror but splintering at a mere rapier's blow. First came Roland, who sat down on his uncle the emperor's right, and then Rinaldo of Montalbano, Astolf, Anjouline of Bayonne, Richard of Normandy and all the others.

At the very end of the table sat Agilulf, still in his stainless battle armor. What had he come to do at table, he who had not and never would have any appetite, nor stomach to fill, nor mouth to bring his fork to, nor palate to sprinkle with Bordeaux wine? Yet he never failed to appear at these banquets, which lasted for hours, though the time would surely have been better employed in operations connected with his duties. But no! He had the right like all the others to a place at the Imperial table, and he occupied it. And he carried out the banquet ceremonial with the same meticulous care that he put into every other ceremonial act of the day.

The courses were the usual ones in a military mess: stuffed turkey roasted on the spit, braised oxen, suckling pig, eels, gold fish. Scarcely had the lackeys offered the platters than the paladins flung themselves on them, rummaged about with their hands and tore the food apart, smearing their cuirasses and squirting sauce everywhere. The confusion was worse than battle—soup tureens overturning, roast chickens flying, and lackeys yanking away platters before a greedy paladin emptied them into his porringer.

At the corner of the table where Agilulf sat, on

the other hand, all proceeded cleanly, calmly and orderly. But he who ate nothing needed more attendance by servers than the whole of the rest of the table. First of all—while there was such a confusion of dirty plates everywhere that there was no chance of changing them between courses and each ate as best he could, even on the tablecloth—Agilulf went on asking to have put in front of him fresh crockery and cutlery, plates big and small, porringers, glasses of every size and shape, innumerable forks and spoons and knives that had to be well sharpened. So exigent was he about cleanliness that a shadow on a glass or plate was enough for him to send it back. He served himself a little of everything. Not a single dish did he let pass. For example, he peeled off a slice of roast boar, put meat on one plate, sauce on another, smaller, plate, then with a very sharp knife chopped the meat into tiny cubes, which one by one he passed on to yet another plate, where he flavored them with sauce, until they were soaked in it. Those with sauce he then put in a new dish and every now and again called a lackey to take away the last plate and bring him a new one. Thus he busied himself for half hours at a time. Not to mention chickens, pheasants, thrushes— at these he worked for whole hours without ever touching them except with the points of little knives, which he asked for specially and which he very often had changed in order to strip the last little bone of its finest and most recalcitrant shred of flesh. He also had wine served, and continuously poured and repoured it among the many beakers and glasses in front of him;

and the goblets in which he mingled one wine with the other he every now and again handed to a lackey to take away and change for a new one. He used a great deal of bread, constantly crushing it into tiny round pellets, all of the same size, which he arranged on the tablecloth in neat rows. The crust he pared down into crumbs, and with them made little pyramids. Eventually he would get tired of them and order the lackeys to brush down the table. Then he started all over again.

With all this he never lost the thread of talk weaving to and fro across the table, and always intervened in time.

What do paladins talk of at dinner? They boast as usual.

Said Roland, "I must tell you that the battle of Aspramonte was going badly before I challenged King Agolante to a duel and bore off Excalibur. So attached to it was he that when I cut off his right arm at a blow, his fist remained tight around its hilt and I had to use pliers to detach 'em."

Said Agilulf, "I do not wish to contradict, but in the interests of accuracy I must record that Excalibur was surrendered by our enemies in accordance with the armistice treaties five days after the battle of Aspramonte. It figures in fact in a list of light weapons handed over to the Frankish army, among the conditions of the treaty."

Exclaimed Rinaldo, "Anyway that's nothing compared with my sword Fusberts. When I met that dragon, passing over the Pyrenees I cut him in two with one blow and, d'you know that a dragon's skin is harder than a diamond?"

Interrupted Agilulf, "One moment, let's just get this clear. The passage of the Pyrenees took place in April, and in April, as everyone knows, dragons slough their skins and are soft and tender as newborn babes."

The paladins said, "Well, yes, that day or another, if not there it was somewhere else, that's what happened, there's no point in splitting hairs . . ."

But they were annoyed. This Agilulf always remembered everything, cited chapter and verse even for a feat of arms accepted by all and piously described by those who had never seen it, tried to reduce it to a normal incident of service to be mentioned in a routine evening's report to a Regimental Commander. Since the world began there has always been a difference between what actually happens in war and what is told afterwards, but it matters little if certain events actually happen or not in a warrior's life. His person, his power, his bearing guarantee that if things did not happen just like that in every petty detail, they might have and still could do so on a similar occasion. But someone like Agilulf has nothing to sustain his own actions, whether true or false. Either they are set down day by day in verbal reports and taken down in registers, or there's emptiness, blankness. He wanted to reduce his colleagues to sponges of Bordeaux wine, full of boasts, of projects winging into the past without ever having been in the present, of legends attributed to different people and eventually hitched to a suitable protagonist.

Every now and again someone would call Charlemagne in testimony. But the emperor had been in so
many wars that he always got confused between one
and another and did not really even remember which
he was fighting now. His job was to wage war, and at
most think of what would come after. Past wars were
neither here nor there to him. Everyone knew that
tales by chroniclers and bards were to be taken with
a grain of salt. The emperor could not be expected to
rectify them all. Only when some matter came up
with repercussions on military organization, on ranks,
for instance, or attribution of titles of nobility or
estates, did the king give an opinion. An opinion of
a sort, of course; in such matters Charlemagne's wishes
counted for little. He had to stick to the issues at
hand, judge by such proofs as were given and see that
laws and customs were respected. So when asked his
opinion he would shrug his shoulders, keep to gener-
alties, and sometimes get out of it with some such
quip as, "Oh! Who knows? War is war, as they say!"
Now on this Sir Agilulf of the Guildivern, who kept
crumbling bread and contradicting all the feats which
—even if not told in versions accurate in every detail
—were genuine glories of Frankish arms, Charlemagne
felt like setting some heavy task, but he had been told
that the knight treated the most tiresome duties as
tests of zeal so there was no point in it.

"I don't see why you must niggle so, Agilulf,"
said Oliver. "The glory of our feats tends to amplify
in the popular memory, thus proving it to be genuine
glory, basis of the titles and ranks we have won."

"Not of mine," rebutted Agilulf. "Every title and predicate of mine I got for deeds well asserted and supported by incontrovertible documentary evidence!"

"So *you* say!" cried a voice.

"Who spoke will answer to me!" said Agilulf, rising to his feet.

"Calm down, now, be good," said the others. "You who are always picking at others' feats, must expect someone to say a word about yours . . ."

"I offend no one. I limit myself to detailing facts, with place, date and proofs!"

"It was I who spoke. I will detail too." A young warrior had got up, pale in the face.

"I'd like to see what you can find contestable in my past, Torrismund," said Agilulf to the youth, who was in fact Torrismund of Cornwall. "Would you deny, for instance, that I was granted my knighthood because, exactly fifteen years ago, I saved from rape by two brigands the King of Scotland's virgin daughter, Sophronia?"

"Yes, I do contest that. Fifteen years ago Sophronia, the King of Scotland's daughter, was no virgin."

A bustle went the whole length of the table. The code of chivalry then holding prescribed that whoever saved from certain danger the virginity of a damsel of noble lineage was immediately dubbed knight. But saving from rape a noblewoman no longer a virgin only brought a mention in despatches and three month's double pay.

"How can you sustain that, which is an affront not only to my dignity as knight but to the lady whom I took under the protection of my sword?"

"I do sustain it."

"Your proof?"

"Sophronia is my mother."

A cry of surprise rose from all the paladins' chests. Was young Torrismund, then, no son of the Duke and Duchess of Cornwall?

"Yes, Sophronia bore me twenty years ago, when she was thirteen years of age," explained Torrismund. "Here is the medal of the royal house of Scotland," and rummaging in his breast he took out a seal on a golden chain.

Charlemagne, who till then had kept his face and beard bent over a dish of river prawns, judged that the moment had come to raise his eyes. "Young knight," said he, giving his voice the major Imperial authority, "do you realise the gravity of your words?"

"Fully," said Torrismund, "for me even more than for others."

There was silence all round. Torrismund was denying a connection to the Duke of Cornwall which bore with it the title of knight. By declaring himself a bastard, even of a princess of blood royal, he risked dismissal from the army.

But much more serious was Agilulf's position. Before battling for Sophronia when she was attacked by bandits, and saving her virtue, he had been a simple nameless warrior in white armor wandering round the world at a venture; or rather (as was soon known) empty white armor, with no warrior inside. His deed in defense of Sophronia had given him the right to be an armed knight. The knighthood of Selimpia Citeriore being vacant just then, he had assumed that title. His entry into service, all ranks and titles added later, were a consequence of that episode. If Sophronia's virginity which he had saved was proved nonexistent, then his knighthood went up in smoke too, and nothing that he had done afterwards could be recognized as valid at all, and his names and titles would be annulled, so that each of his attributions would become as nonexistent as his person.

"When still a child, my mother became pregnant with me," narrated Torrismund, "and fearing the ire of her parents when they knew her state, fled from the royal castle of Scotland and wandered throughout the highlands. She gave birth to me in the open air, on a heath, and while wandering over fields and woods of England raised me till I was five. Those first memories are of the loveliest period of my life, interrupted by this intruder. I remember the day. My mother had left me to guard our cave, while she went off as usual to rob fruit from the orchards. She met two roving brigands who wanted to abuse her. They might have made friends in the end, who knows, for my mother often lamented her solitude. Then along came this empty armor in search of glory and routed the brigands. Recognizing my mother as of royal blood, he took her under his protection and brought her to the nearest castle, that of Cornwall, where he consigned her to the duke and duchess. Meanwhile I had remained in the cave hungry and alone. As soon as my mother could she confessed to the duke and duchess the existence of her son whom she had been forced to abandon. Servants bearing torches were sent out to search for me and I was brought to the castle. To save the honor of the royal family of Scotland, linked to that of Cornwall by bonds of kinship, I was adopted and recognized as son of the duke and duchess. My life was tedious and burdened with restriction as the lives of cadets of noble houses always are. No longer was I allowed to see my mother, who took the veil in a distant convent. This mountain of falsehood has weighed me down and distorted the natural course of my life. Now finally I have succeeded in telling the truth. Whatever happens to me now must be better than the past."

At table meanwhile the pudding had been served, a sponge in various delicately colored layers, but such was the general amazement at this series of revelations that not a fork was raised towards speechless mouths.

"And you, what have you to say about this story?" Charlemagne asked Agilulf. All noted that he had not said, "Knight."

"Lies. Sophronia was a virgin. On the flower of her purity repose my honor and my name."

"Can you prove it?"

"I will search out Sophronia."

"Do you expect to find her the same fifteen years later?" said Astolfo maliciously. "Breastplates of beaten iron have lasted less."

"She took the veil immediately after I had consigned her to that pious family."

"In fifteen years, in times like these, no convent

in Christendom has been saved from dispersal and sack, and every nun has had time to de-nun and re-nun herself at least four or five times over."

"Anyway, violated chastity presupposes a violator. I will find him and obtain proof from him of the date when Sophronia could be considered a virgin."

"I give you permission to leave this instant, should you so desire," said the emperor. "I feel that nothing at this moment can be closer to your heart than the right to wear a name and arms now contested. If what this young man says is true I cannot keep you in my service. In fact I can take no account of you, even to make good arrears of pay," and here Charlemagne could not prevent giving a touch of passing satisfaction to his little speech as if to say, "At last we've found a way of getting rid of this bore!"

The white armor now leant forward, and never till that moment had it shown itself so empty. The voice issuing from it was scarcely audible. "Yes, my Emperor, I will go."

"And you?" Charlemagne turned to Torrismund. "Do you realize that by declaring yourself born out of wedlock you cannot bear the rank due to your birth? Do you at least know who was your father? And have you any hope of his recognizing you?"

"I can never be recognized . . ."

"One never knows. Every man, when growing older, tends to make out a balance sheet of his whole life. I too have recognized all my children by concubines, and there were many, some certainly not mine at all."

"My father was no man."

"And who was he? Beelzebub?"

"No, sire," said Torrismund calmly.

"Who then?"

Torrismund moved to the middle of the hall, put a knee to the ground, raised his eyes to the sky and said, " 'Tis the Sacred Order of the Knights of the Holy Grail!"

A murmur rustled over the banqueting table. One or two of the paladins crossed themselves.

"My mother was a bold lass," explained Torrismund, "and always ran into the deepest woods around the castle. One day in the thick of the forest she met the Knights of the Holy Grail, encamped there to fortify their spirit in isolation from the world. The child began playing with those warriors and from that day she went to their camp every time she could elude family surveillance. But in a short time she returned pregnant from those childish games."

Charlemagne remained in thought a moment, then said, "The Knights of the Holy Grail have all made a vow of chastity and none of them can ever recognize you as a son."

"Nor would I wish them to," said Torrismund. "My mother has never spoken of any knight in particular, but brought me up to respect as a father the Sacred Order as a whole."

"Then," added Charlemagne, "the Order as a whole is not bound by any vow of the kind. Nothing therefore prevents it from being recognized as a person's father. If you succeed in finding the Knights of the Holy Grail and get them to recognize you as son of the whole Order collectively, then your military rights, in view of the Order's prerogatives, would be no different from those you had as scion of a noble house."

"I go," said Torrismund.

It was an evening of departure, that night, in the Frankish camp. Agilulf prepared his baggage and horse meticulously, and his squire Gurduloo rolled up in knapsacks blankets, currycombs, caldrons, which made such a heap they prevented his seeing where he was riding. He took the opposite direction to his master and galloped off, losing everything on the way.

No one had come to greet Agilulf as he left, except a few poor ostlers and blacksmiths who did not make too many distinctions and realized this officer might be fussier but was also unhappier than others. The paladins did not come, with the excuse that they did not know the time of his departure and anyway there was no reason to. Agilulf had not said a word to any of them since coming from the banquet. His departure aroused no comment. When his duties were distributed in such a way that none remained unaccounted for, the absence of the nonexistent knight was thought best left in silence by general consent.

The ony one to be moved, indeed overwhelmed, was Bradamante. She hurried to her tent. "Quick!" she called to her maids and retainers, "Quick!" and flung into the air clothes, armor, lances and orna-

ments, "Quick!" doing this not as usual when un-
dressing or angry, but to have all put in order, make
an inventory and leave. "Prepare everything, I'm
leaving, leaving, not staying here another minute; he's
gone. The only one who made any sense in this whole
army, the only one who can give any sense to my life
and my war, and now there's nothing left but a bunch
of louts and nincompoops including myself, and
life is just a constant rolling between bed and battle.
He alone knew the secret geometry, the order, the
rule, by which to understand its beginning and end!"
So saying, she put on her country armor piece by piece,
and over it her periwinkle robe. Soon she was in
the saddle, male in all except the proud way certain
true women have of looking virile, spurred her horse
to the gallop, dragging down palisades and tents and
sausage stalls, and soon vanished into a high cloud
of dust.

That dust was seen by Raimbaut as he ran about
on foot looking for her, crying, "Where are you
going, oh, where Bradamante. Here am I for you,
for you, and you go away!" with a lover's stubborn
indignation which means, "I'm here, girl, loaded with
love, how can you not want it, what *can* a girl want
that she doesn't take me, doesn't love me, what can
she want more than what I feel I can and ought to
give?" So he rages, incapable of accepting rejection;
at a certain moment love for her becomes love of
himself, love of himself is love for her and for what
could be for them both and is not. And in his frenzy
Raimbaut ran into his tent, prepared horse, arms and

knapsack, and left too. For war can be well fought where there's a glimpse of a woman's mouth between lance points. Nothing—wounds, dust, the stink of a horse—means anything but that smile.

Torrismund also left that evening, sad and hopeful too. He wanted to find the wood again, the damp dark wood of his infancy, his mother, his days in that cave, and even more, the pure comradeship of his fathers, armed and watching around a hidden bivouac fire, robed in white, silent in the thick of a forest, with low branches almost touching bracken and mushrooms sprouting from rich earth which never saw sun.

Charlemagne, as he rose from the banquet, rather shaky on his legs, heard of all these sudden departures and moved towards the royal pavilion thinking of days when the departures were of Astolf, Rinaldo, Guidon Selvaggio, Roland, to do deeds which later entered the epics of poets, while now the same veterans would never move a step unless forced by duty. "Let them go, they're young, let them get on with it," said Charlemagne, with the habit, usual to men of action, of considering movement always good, but already with the bitterness of the old who suffer at losing things of the past more than they enjoy greeting those of the future.

{ 8 }

BOOK, evening is here, and I have begun to write more rapidly. No sound now rises from the river but the rumble of the cascade; bats fly mutely by the window, a dog bays, voices ring from the haystacks. Maybe this penance of mine has not been so ill chosen by the Mother Abbess. Every now and again I notice by pen beginning to hurry over the paper as if by itself, with my hurrying along after it. 'Tis towards the truth we hurry, my pen and I, the truth which I am constantly expecting to meet deep in a white page, and which I can reach only when my pen strokes have succeeded in burying all the disgust and dissatisfaction and rancor which I am forced here in seclusion to expiate.

Then at a mere scamper of a mouse (the convent attics are full of them), or a sudden gust of wind banging the shutter (always apt to distract me, and I hurry to reopen it), or at the end of some episode in this tale and the start of another, or maybe just at the repetition of a line, my pen is heavy as a cross once again and my race towards truth wavers in its course.

Now I must show the lands crossed by Agilulf and his squire on their journey. I must set it all down on this page, a dusty main road, a river, a bridge, and Agilulf passing on his light-hooved horse, toc-toc toc-toc, for this knight without a body weighs little, and the horse can do many a mile without tiring and its master is quite untirable. Next a heavy gallop passes over the bridge: tututum! It's Gurduloo clutching the neck of his horse, their two heads so close it's impossible to tell if the horse is thinking with the squire's head or the squire with the horse's. On my paper I trace a straight line with occasional curves, and this is Agilulf's route. This other line all twirls and zigzags is Gurduloo's. When he sees a butterfly flutter by, Gurduloo at once urges his horse after it, thinking himself astride not the horse but the butterfly, and so wanders off the road and into the fields. Meanwhile Agilulf goes straight ahead, following his course. Every now and again Gurduloo's route off the road coincides with invisible short cuts (or maybe the horse is following a path of its own choice, with no guidance from its rider) and after many a twist and turn the vagabond finds himself again beside his master on the main road.

Here on the river's bank I will set a mill. Agilulf stops to ask the way. The miller woman replies courteously and offers wine and bread, which he refuses. He accepts only fodder for the horse. The road is dusty and sun-swept. The good millers are amazed at the knight's not being thirsty.

When he has just left, up gallops Gurduloo, with the sound of a regiment at full tilt. "Have you seen my master?"

"And who may your master be?"

"A knight . . . no, a horse . . ."

"Are you in a horse's service then?"

"No . . . it's my horse that's in a horse's service . . ."

"Who's riding that horse?"

"Eh . . . no one knows . . ."

"Who is riding your own horse, then?"

"Oh, ask it!"

"Don't you want any food or drink either?"

"Yes, yes! Eat! Drink!" and he gulps it all down.

Now I am drawing a town girt with walls. Agilulf has to pass through it. The guards at the gate ask him to show his face. They have orders to let no one pass with closed visor, lest he be a ferocious brigand infesting the local countryside. Agilulf refuses, comes to blows with the guard, forces his passage, escapes.

Beyond the town I now trace out a wood. Agilulf scours it through and through until he finds the dreadful bandit. He disarms him, chains him up, and drags him before the guards who had refused him passage. "Here is the man you so much feared!"

"Ah blessings on you, white knight! But tell us who you are, and why you keep your helmet shut?"

"My name is at my journey's end," says Agilulf, and flees.

Around the town goes a rumor that he is an archangel or soul from purgatory. "The horse moved so lightly," says one, "there might have been no one in the saddle at all."

Here by the edge of the wood passes another road also leading to the town. Along this road is riding Bradamante. To those in the town she says, "I am looking for a knight in white armor. I know him to be here."

"No. No, he's not," is the reply.

"If he's not, then it must be him."

"Go and find where he is, then. He's rushed away from here."

"Have you really seen him? White armor which seems to have a man inside?"

"Who's inside if not a man?"

"One who is more than all other men!"

"There's devil's work in this," says an old man, "and in you too. O knight of the gentle voice!"

Away spurs Brandamante.

A little later, Raimbaut reins his horse in the town square. "Have you seen a knight pass?"

"Which? Two have passed and you're the third."

"One rushing after the other."

"Is it true one isn't a man?"

"The second is a woman."

"And the first?"

"Nothing."

"What about you?"

"Me? I'm . . . I'm a man."

"Thanks be to God!"

Agilulf was riding along, followed by Gurduloo. A damsel ran onto the road, with flowing hair and tattered dress, and flung herself on her knees. Agilulf stopped his horse. "Help, noble cavalier," she invoked. "Half a mile from here a flock of wild bears is besieging the castle of my lady, the noble widow Priscilla. Only a few helpless women inhabit the castle. Nobody can get in or out. I was dropped by a rope from the battlements and escaped the claws of those beasts by a miracle. O knight, come and free us, do!"

"My sword is always at the service of widows and helpless creatures," said Agilulf. "Gurduloo, take on your crupper this damsel who will guide us to the castle of her mistress."

They began climbing a rocky path. The squire was not even looking at the way as he rode; the breast of the woman sitting in his arms showed pink and plump through the tears in her dress, and Gurduloo felt lost.

The damsel turned to look at Agilulf. "What a noble bearing your master has!" she said.

"Uh, uh," replied Gurduloo, reaching out a hand towards that warm breast.

"He's so sure and proud in every word and gesture . . ." said she, still with eyes on Agilulf.

"Uh," exclaimed Gurduloo as, his rein slung on his wrist, he tried with both hands to ascertain how a creature could be so steady and soft at the same time.

"And his voice," said she, "so sharp and metallic . . ."

From Gurduloo's mouth came only a faint whine,

for he had buried it between the young woman's neck and shoulder and was lost in their scent.

"How happy my mistress will be to find herself freed from the bears by such a man . . . Oh I do envy her . . . But hey, we're going off the track! What is it, squire, are you distracted?"

At a turn in the path was a hermit, holding out a hand for alms. Agilulf, who gave to every beggar he met the regular sum of three centimes, drew in his horse and rummaged in his purse.

"Blessings on you, knight," said the hermit pocketing the money, and signing for him to bend down so as to speak in his ear, "I will reward you at once by telling you to beware of the widow Priscilla! This tale of the bears is all a trap. She herself raises them, so as to be freed by the most valiant knights passing on the road below and draw them up to the castle to feed her insatiable lust."

"It may be as you say, brother," replied Agilulf, "but I am a knight and it would be discourteous to reject a formal request for help made by a female in tears."

"Are you not afraid of the flames of lust?"

Agilulf was slightly embarrassed. "Well, we'll see . . ."

"Do you know what remains of a knight after a sojourn in that castle?"

"What?"

"You see it before your eyes. I too was a knight. I too saved Priscilla from the bears, and now here I am!" And he really was in rather bad shape.

"I will take note of your experience, brother, but I affront the trial," and Agilulf spurred away and up to Gurduloo and the girl.

"I don't know what these hermits always find to gossip about," said the girl to the knight. "No group of religious or lay folk chatter so much and so maliciously."

"Are there many hermits round here?"

"It's full of 'em. And new ones are constantly being added."

"I will not be one of those," exclaimed Agilulf. "Let's hurry!"

"I hear the snarl of bears," exclaimed the girl. "I'm afraid! Let me get down and hide behind that bush!"

Agilulf came out onto the open space before the castle. Everything was black with bears. At the sight of horse and knight they bared their teeth and lined up side by side to bar his way. Agilulf set his lance and charged. One or two he pierced, others he stunned, others he bruised. Gurduloo came riding up and chased them with a kitchen spit. In ten minutes those not stretched on the ground like so many carpets had gone to hide in the forest depths.

The castle gate opened. "Noble knight, can hospitality repay what I owe you?" On the threshold had appeared Priscilla, surrounded by her ladies and maids. Among these was the young woman who had accompanied the pair till then. Inexplicably, she was already home and no longer dressed in rags but a nice clean apron.

Agilulf, followed by Gurduloo, made his entry into the castle. The widow Priscilla was not tall and not short, not plump but well contained, with a bosom not large but well in view, and sparkling black eyes, in fact a woman with something to say for herself. There she stood, before Agilulf's white armor, looking pleased. The knight was grave but reserved.

"Sir Agilulf Emo Bertrandin of the Guildivern," said Priscilla, "I know your name already and know who you are and who you are *not*."

At this announcement Agilulf, as if freed from a discomfort, put aside his shyness and looked more at ease. Even so he bowed, dropped on one knee, and said, "At your service," then jumped to his feet with a start.

"I have heard you much spoken of," said Priscilla, "and it has been for long my ardent wish to meet you. What miracle has brought you along this remote road?"

"I am travelling," said Agilulf, "to trace, before it be too late, a virginity of fifteen years ago."

"Never have I heard a knightly enterprise with so fleeting an aim," said Priscilla. "But as fifteen years have passed I have no scruples in retarding you another night, and requesting you to be a guest in my castle," and off she moved beside him.

The other women all stood there with eyes fixed on him until he vanished with the chatelaine into a series of withdrawing chambers. Then they turned to Gurduloo.

"Aha, what a fine figure of a squire," they cried,

clapping their hands. He stood there like an ape, scratching himself. "A pity he has so many fleas and stinks so," they said. "Quick, let's wash him!" They bore him to their quarters and stripped him naked.

Priscilla had led Agilulf to a table laid for two. "I know your habitual temperance, knight," said she, "but how else can I begin to do you honor but by inviting you to sit at my board? Certainly," she added slyly, "the signs of gratitude which I intend to offer do not stop there!"

Agilulf thanked her, sat down facing the chatelaine, broke a few pieces of bread in his fingers, and after a moment or two of silence, cleared his voice and began to converse fluently.

"How truly strange and eventful, lady, are the adventures which befall a knight errant. These can be grouped under various headings. First . . ." And so he conversed, affably, clearly, informatively, at times arousing a suspicion of overmeticulousness, soon banished by the volubility with which he went on to other subjects, interlarding serious phrases with jests in excellent taste, expressing about matters and persons opinions neither too favorable nor too contrary, and always such as to offer his partner opportunities to voice her own opinions, and encouraging her with gracious questions.

"Oh, what delicious talk is this!" exclaimed Priscilla, beaming.

Then just as suddenly as he had begun talking Agilulf went silent.

"Let the singing begin," cried Priscilla, and

clapped her hands. Lute girls entered the chamber. One intoned the song which starts, " 'Tis the unicorn gathers the rose"; then another, *"Jasmin, veulliez embellir le beau coussin."*

Agilulf had words of appreciation for both music and voices.

Now a cluster of maidens entered dancing. They wore tight robes and had garlands in their hair. Agilulf accompanied their dance by banging his iron gloves on the table in rhythm.

No less festive were the dances taking place in another wing of the castle, in the quarters of the maidens in waiting. Half clothed, the young women were playing at ball and drawing Gurduloo into the game. The squire, dressed in a short tunic which the ladies had lent him, never kept to his place or waited for the ball to be thrown but ran after it and tried to grasp it in any way he could, flinging himself head-long at one or another damsel, then amid his struggles being often struck by another inspiration and rolling with the girl on one of the soft cushions scattered around.

"Oh, what *are* you doing? Oh no, no, you great big camel! Oh, see what he's doing to me! No, I want to play ball. Ah! ah! ah!"

Gurduloo was quite beside himself now. What with the warm bath they had given him, the scents and all that pink and white flesh, his only desire now was to merge into the general fragrance.

"Oh oh, here again. Oh, my God! Oh really, aah . . . !"

The others went on playing ball as if noticing nothing, jesting, laughing and singing. "Oho! Ohi! The moon does fly on high . . ."

The girl whom Gurduloo had whisked away, after a long last cry, returned to her companions rather flushed, rather stunned, then laughing and clapping her hands cried, "Over here, here to me!" and began to play again.

Before long Gurduloo was rolling on another girl.

"Come on, come on, oh what a bore, oh what a thruster, no, you're hurting . . ." and she succumbed.

Other women and maidens not participating in the game were sitting on benches and chattering away . . . "Since Philomena, you know, was jealous of Clara, but . . ." then one would suddenly feel herself seized round the waist by Gurduloo . . . "Oh, what a fright! . . . well, as I was saying, William seems to have gone with Euphemia . . . where *are* you taking me?" Gurduloo had loaded her onto a shoulder . . . "D'you understand? Meanwhile that other silly with her usual jealousy . . ." The girl was continuing to chatter and gesticulate as, dangling on Gurduloo's shoulder, she vanished.

Not long after, back she came, rather dishevelled, a shoulder strap torn which she settled back, still gabbing away, "Well, as I was saying, Philomena made such a scene with Clara, and the other, on the other hand . . ."

In the banqueting chamber dancers and songsters had withdrawn. Agilulf was giving the chatelaine a long list of compositions often played by the Emperor Charlemagne's musicians.

"The sky darkens," observed Priscilla.

" 'Tis night, deep night," admitted Agilulf.

"The room which I have reserved for you . . ."

"Thanks. Listen to the nightingale out there in the park."

"The room which I have reserved for you . . . is my own . . ."

"Your hospitality is exquisite . . . 'Tis from that oak the nightingale sings. Let us draw close to the window."

He got up, offered her his iron arm, moved to the window. The gurgle of nightingales was a cue for him to launch out on a series of poetic and mythological references.

But Priscilla cut this off short. "What the nightingale sings about is love. And we . . ."

"Ah love!" cried Agilulf with such a brusque change of tone that Priscilla was alarmed. Then, without a break, he plunged into a dissertation of the passion of love. Priscilla was tenderly excited. Leaning on his arm, she urged him towards a room dominated by a big four-poster bed.

"Among the ancients, as love was considered a god . . ." Agilulf was pouring out.

Priscilla closed the door with a double bolt, went up to him, bowed her head on his armor and said, "I'm a little cold, the fire is spent . . ."

"The opinion of the ancients," said Agilulf, "as to whether it be better to make love in cold rooms rather than in hot is a controversial one. But the advice of most . . ."

"Oh, you do know all about love," whispered Priscilla.

"The advice of most is against stiflingly hot rooms and in favor of a certain natural warmth."

"Shall I call my maidens, to light the fire?"

"I will light it myself." He examined the wood in the fireplace, praised the flame of this or that type of wood, enumerated the various ways of lighting fires in the open or in enclosed places. A sigh from Priscilla interrupted him. As if realizing that this new subject was dispersing the amorous atmosphere being created, Agilulf quickly began smattering his speech with references and allusions and comparisons to warmth of emotions and senses.

Priscilla, smiling now, with half-closed eyes, stretching out a hand towards the flames which were beginning to crackle, said, "How lovely and warm . . . how sweet it would be to be warm between sheets, prone . . ."

The mention of bed suggested a series of new observations to Agilulf; according to him the difficult art of bed making was unknown to the serving maids of France, and in nobles' palaces could be found only ill-stretched sheets.

"Oh no, do tell me, my bed too . . . ?" asked the widow.

"Certainly yours is a queen's bed, superior to all others in the Imperial dominions, but my desire to see you surrounded only with things worthy of you ın every detail makes me eye that fold there with some apprehension . . ."

"Oh, a fold!" cried Priscilla, also swept by the passion for perfection communicated to her by Agilulf.

They undid the bed, finding and deploring little folds and puckers, portions too stretched or too loose, and this search gave moments of stabbing anguish and others of ascent to ever higher skies.

Having upset the whole bed as far as the mattress, Agilulf began to remake it according to the rules. This was an elaborate operation. Nothing was to be left to chance, and secret expedients were put to work. All this with diffuse explanations to the widow. But every now and again something left him dissatisfied, and he would begin all over again.

From the other wings of the castle rang a cry, or rather a moan or bray, forced out unwillingly.

"What's that?" started Priscilla.

"Nothing, it's my squire's voice," said he.

With that shout mingled others more acute, like strident sighs soaring to the sky.

"What's that now?" asked Agilulf.

"Oh, just the girls," said Priscilla. "Playing . . . youth, you know."

And they went on remaking the bed, listening every now and again to the sounds of the night.

"Gurduloo's shouting . . ."

"What a noise those girls do make . . ."

"The nightingale."

"The cicadas . . ."

The bed was now ready, puckerless. Agilulf turned

towards the widow. She was naked. Her robes had fallen chastely to the floor.

"Naked ladies are advised," declared Agilulf, "that the most sublime of sensual emotions is embracing a warrior in full armor."

"You don't need to teach me that!" exclaimed Priscilla. "I wasn't born yesterday!" So saying, she took a leap and clamped herself to Agilulf, entwining her legs and arms around his armor.

One after the other she tried all the ways in which armor can be embraced, then, all langor, entered the bed.

Agilulf knelt down beside her pillow. "Your hair," he said.

Priscilla when disrobing had not undone the high array of her brown mane of hair. Agilulf began illustrating the place of loose hair in the transport of the senses. "Let's try."

With firm delicate movements of his iron hands he loosened her castle of tresses and made her hair fall down over her breast and shoulders.

"But," he added, "it is certainly more subtle for a man to prefer a woman whose body is naked but hair elaborately dressed, even covered with veils and diadems."

"Shall we try again?"

"I will dress your hair myself." He dressed it and showed his capacity at weaving tresses, winding and twisting them round and fixing them with big pins. Then he made an elaborate arrangement of veils and jewels. So an hour passed, but Priscilla, on his handing her the mirror, had never seen herself so lovely.

She invited him to lie down by her side. "They say," said he, "that every night Cleopatra dreamt she had an armed warrior in her bed."

"I've never tried," she confessed, "they usually take it off beforehand."

"Well, try now." And slowly, without soiling the sheets, he entered the bed fully armed from head to foot and stretched out taut as if on a tomb.

"Don't you even loosen the sword from its scabbard?"

"Amorous passion knows no half measures."

Priscilla shut her eyes in ecstasy.

Agilulf raised himself on an elbow. "The fire is smoking. I will get up to see why the flue does not draw."

The moon was just showing at the window. On his way back from fireplace to bed Agilulf paused. "Lady, let us go out onto the battlements and enjoy this late moonlit eve."

He wrapped her in his cloak. Entwined, they climbed the tower. The moon silvered the forest. A horned owl sang. Some windows of the castle were still alight and from them every now and again came cries or laughs or groans or a bray from the squire.

"All nature is love . . ."

They returned to the room. The fire was almost out. They crouched down to puff on the embers. Now that they were close to each other, with Priscilla's pink knee grazing his metallic greave, a new, more innocent intimacy grew.

When Priscilla went to bed again the window was already touched by first light. "Nothing disfigures a woman's face like the first ray of dawn," said Agilulf. But to get her face to appear in the best light he had to move bed, posts and all.

"How do I look?" asked the widow.

"Most lovely."

Priscilla was happy. But the sun was rising fast and to follow its rays Agilulf continually had to move the bed.

" 'Tis dawn," said he. His voice had already changed. "My duty as knight requires me to set out on my road at this hour."

"Already!" moaned Priscilla.

"I regret, gentle lady, but 'tis a graver duty urges me."

"Oh how lovely it was . . ."

Agilulf bent his knee. "Bless me, Priscilla." He rose, called his squire. He had to wander all over the castle before he finally spied him, exhausted, asleep like a log in a kind of dog kennel. "Quick, saddle up!" but he had to carry Gurduloo himself. The sun in its continuing ascent outlined the two figures on horseback against golden leaves in the woods—the squire balanced like a sack, the knight straight, pollarded like the slim shadow of a poplar.

Maidens and servant maids had hurried around Priscilla.

"How was it, mistress, how was it?"

"Oh, if you only knew! What a man, what a man . . ."

"But do tell, do describe, how was it? Tell us."

"A man . . . a man . . . a knight . . . a continuous
. . . a paradise . . ."

"But what did he *do*? What did he *do*?"

"How can one tell that? Oh, lovely, how lovely
it was . . ."

"But has he got everything? Yet . . . Do tell . . ."

"I simply wouldn't know now . . . So much . . .
But what about you, with that squire . . . ?"

"Oh, nothing, no, did you? No, you? I really forget . . ."

"What? I could hear you, my dears . . ."

"Oh well, poor boy, I don't remember, I don't
remember either, may you . . . what, me? Mistress,
do tell us about him, about the knight, eh? What
was Agilulf like?"

"Oh, Agilulf!"

{ 9 }

AS I write this book, following a tale told in an ancient almost illegible chronicle, I realise only now that I have filled page after page and am still at the very beginning. For now the real ramifications of the plot get under way: Agilulf and his squire's intrepid journey for proof of Sophronia's virginity, interwoven with Bradamante's pursuit and flight, Raimbaut's love, and Torrismund's search for the Knights of the Grail. But this thread, instead of running swiftly through my fingers, is apt to sag or stick and when I think of all the journeys and obstacles and flights and deceits and duels and jousts that I still have to put on paper I feel rather dazed. How this discipline as convent scribe and my assiduous penance of seeking words and all my meditations on ultimate truths have changed me. What the vulgar—and I too till now—considered as the greatest of delights, the interweaving adventures which make up every knightly tale, now seem to me pointless decoration, mere fringe, the hardest part of my task.

I long to hurry on with my story, tell it quickly,

embellish every page with enough duels and battles for a poem but when I pause and start rereading I realise that my pen has left no mark on the paper and the pages are blank.

To tell it as I would like, this blank page would have to bristle with reddish rocks, flake with pebbly sand, spout sparse juniper trees. In the midst of a twisting ill-marked track, I would set Agilulf, passing erect on his saddle, lance at rest. But this page would have to be not only a rocky slope but the dome of sky above, slung so low that there is room only for a flight of cawing rooks in between. With my pen I should also trace faint dents in the paper to represent the slither of an invisible snake through grass or a hare crossing a heath, suddenly coming into the clear, stopping, sniffing around through its short whiskers, then vanishing again.

Everything moves on this bare page with no sign, no change on its surface, as after all everything moves and nothing changes on the earth's crinkly crust; for there is but one single expanse of the same material, as there is with the sheet on which I write, an expanse which in spite of contractions and congealings in different forms and consistencies and various subtle colorings can still seem smeared over a flat surface. And even when hairy or feathery or knobbly bits seem at various times to move, that is but the change between the relations of various qualities distributed over the expanse of uniform matter, without anything changing in fact. The only person who can be said definitely to be on the move is

Agilulf, by which I do not mean his horse or armor, but that lonely self-preoccupied, impatient something jogging along on horseback inside the armor. Around him pine cones fall from branches, streams gurgle over pebbles, fish swim in streams, maggots gnaw at leaves, tortoises rub their hard bellies on the ground, but all this is mere illusion of movement, perpetual revolving to and fro like waves. And in this wave Gurduloo is revolving to and fro, prisoner of the world's stuff, he too smeared like the pine cones, fish, maggots, stones and leaves, a mere excrescence on the earth's crust.

How much more difficult it is for me to plot on my paper Bradamante's course or Raimbaut's or glum Torrismund's! There would have to be some very faint pucker on the surface as can be got by pricking paper from below with a pin, and this pucker would always have to be impregnated with the general matter of the world and this itself constitute its sense and beauty and sorrow, its true attrition and movement.

But how can I get on with my tale, if I begin to torture the white page like this, scoop out valleys and clefts in it, score it with creases and scratches, reading into it the paladin's progress? To help tell my tale it would be better if I drew a map, the gentle countryside of France, and proud Brittany, and the English Channel surging with black billows, and high Scotland up there and harsh Pyrenees down here, and Spain still in Infidel hands, and Africa mother of serpents. Then with arrows and crosses and numbers I could plot the journey of one or other of our heroes. Here, for instance, with a rapid line in spite of a few twists I can make Agilulf land in England and direct him towards the convent where Sophronia has lived, retired, for fifteen years.

He arrives, and finds the convent a mass of ruins.

"You come too late, noble knight," said an old man. "These valleys still resound with the cries of those poor women. A short while ago a fleet of Moorish pirates landed on this coast and sacked the convent, bore off the nuns as slaves and set fire to the walls."

"Bore off, where to?"

"As slaves to be sold in Morocco, m'lord."

"Was there among those nuns one Sophronia, who in the world was the King of Scotland's daughter?"

"Ah, you mean Sister Palmyra! There was indeed! They loaded her up on their shoulders straight away, the rascals! Though no longer a girl she was still attractive. I remember as if it were now, her shouts and groans at those ugly faces."

"Were you present at the sack?"

"Well, we who live here, you know, are always out on the green."

"And you didn't help?"

"Help who? Well m'lord, you know, so suddenly . . . we had no orders, or experience . . . Between doing a thing and doing it badly we thought it best to do nothing at all."

"Tell me, did this Sophronia lead a pious life in the convent?"

"These days there are nuns of all kinds, but Sister

Palmyra was the holiest and most chaste in the entire diocese."

"Quick, Gurduloo, down to the port we go and embark for Morocco."

All this part I am now scoring with wavy lines is the sea, or rather the ocean. Now I draw the ship on which Agilulf makes his journey, and further on I draw an enormous whale, with an ornamental scroll and the words "Ocean Sea." This arrow indicates the ship's route. I do another arrow showing the whale's course: there, they met. So at this point of the ocean will take place an encounter between whale and ship, and as I've drawn the whale in bigger, the ship will get the worst of it. Now I'm drawing in a crisscross of arrows to show that at this point there was a savage battle between whale and ship. Agilulf fights peerlessly and plunges his lance into the creature's side. Over him squirts a nauseating jet of whale oil, which I show by these divergent lines. Gurduloo leaps onto the whale and forgets all about the ship, which at a whisk from the whale's tail overturns. Agilulf with his iron armor of course sinks like a stone. Before the waves entirely submerge him he cries to his squire, "We'll meet in Morocco! I'm walking there!"

In fact, after dropping mile after mile into the depths, Agilulf lands on his feet on the sand at the bottom of the sea and begins walking briskly. Often he meets marine monsters and defends himself against them with his sword. The only bother about armor at the bottom of the sea is rust. But having been squirted from head to foot in whale oil, the white armor has a layer of grease which keeps it intact.

On the ocean I now draw a turtle. Gurduloo has gulped down a pint of salty water before realising that the sea is not supposed to be inside him but he inside the sea. Eventually he seizes the shell of a big sea turtle. Partly letting himself be drawn along, partly guiding it by pinches and prods, he and the turtle near the coast of Africa. Here they become entangled in the nets of some Moorish fishermen.

When the nets are drawn on board the fishermen see amid a wriggling school of mullet a man in soaking wet clothes covered with seaweed. "The merman! The merman!" they cry.

"Merman? Nonsense! It's Gudi-Ussuf," cries the head fisherman. "It's Gudi-Ussuf, I know him!"

Gudi-Ussuf was in fact one of the names by which Gurduloo was known in the Moslem field kitchens, when unsuspectingly he crossed the lines and found himself in the Sultan's camp. The head fisherman had been a trooper in the Moorish army in Spain, so knowing Gurduloo to have a strong body and docile mind, he took him on as an oyster fisher.

One evening the fishermen, and Gurduloo among them, were sitting on the rocky Moroccan shore opening the oysters they'd fished one by one, when from the water appeared a helmet, a breastplate, and then a complete suit of armor walking step by step up the beach. "A lobster man! A lobster man!" cried the fishermen—running away in terror to hide among the rocks.

"A lobster man! Nonsense!" said Gurduloo. "It's my master! You must be exhausted, sir, after walking all that way!"

"I'm not the least tired," replied Agilulf. "And you? What are you doing here?"

"Finding pearls for the Sultan," intervened the ex-soldier, "as he has to give a new pearl to a different wife every night."

Having three hundred and sixty-five wives, the Sultan visited one a night, so every wife was only visited once a year. To the one visited it was his custom to give a pearl, so that every day merchants had to supply him with a fresh new pearl. As that day the merchants had exhausted their supplies, they had recourse to the fishermen to procure a pearl at all costs.

"You who've managed to walk so well on the sea bottom," the ex-soldier said to Agilulf, "why don't you join our enterprise?"

"Knights do not join enterprises with lucre as their aim, particularly if conducted by enemies of his religion. I thank you, O Pagan, for having saved and fed this squire of mine, but I don't care a jot if your Sultan cannot present a pearl to this three hundred and sixty-fifth wife tonight."

"We care a lot, though, as we shall all be whipped," exclaimed the fisherman. "Tonight is no ordinary wife's night. It's the turn of a new one, whom the Sultan is visiting for the first time. She was bought almost a year ago from certain pirates, and has awaited her turn till now. 'Tis improper that the Sultan should present himself to her with empty hands, particularly as she is a coreligionist of yours, Sophronia of Scotland, of royal blood brought to Morocco as a slave and immediately destined for our sovereign's harem."

Agilulf did not betray his emotion. "I will show you how to get out of your difficulty," said he. "Let the merchants suggest that the Sultan bring his new wife not the usual pearl but a present to soothe her homesickness: the complete armor of a Christian warrior."

"Where can we find such armor?"

"Mine!" said Agilulf.

Sophronia was awaiting nightfall in her quarters of the palace harem. From the grating of the cusped window she looked out over garden palms, fountains, alleys. The sun was setting, the muezzin launching his cry, and in the garden the scented flowers of dusk were opening.

A knock. 'Tis time! No, the usual eunuchs. They are bearing a present from the Sultan. A suit of armor. Of white armor. What can it mean? Sophronia, alone again, remains at the window. She has been there for almost a year. When bought as a wife she had been assigned the place of a wife recently repudiated, a place which would fall due again more than eleven months later. Living in the harem doing nothing, one day after the other, was even more boring than life in the convent had been.

"Do not fear, noble Sophronia," said a voice behind her. She turned. It was the armor talking. "I am Agilulf of the Guildivern who saved your immaculate virtue once before."

"Help!" screamed the Sultan's wife. Then, recomposing herself, "Ah yes, I thought I knew that white armor. It was you who arrived just in time, years ago, to prevent me from being abused by a brigand . . ."

"Now I arrive just in time to save you from the horror of pagan nuptials."

"Oh yes . . . Always you . . . you are . . ."

"Now, protected by this sword, I will accompany you forth from the Sultan's domains."

"Yes . . . indeed . . . of course."

When the eunuchs came to announce the Sultan's arrival they were put to the sword one by one. Wrapped in a cloak, Sophronia ran through the gardens by the knight's side. The dragomen gave the alarm. But their heavy scimitars could do little against the agile sword of the warrior in white armor. And his shield sustained well the assault of a whole picket's lances. Gurduloo was waiting behind a cactus tree with horses. In the port a felucca was ready to leave for Christian lands. From the prow Sophronia watched the palms of the beach drawing further away.

Now I am drawing the felucca here in the sea. I'm doing a rather bigger one than the ship before, so that if it does meet a whale there'll be no disaster. With this curved line I mark the passage of the felucca which I want to reach the port of St. Malo. The trouble is that here in the Bay of Biscay there's such a mess of crisscrossing lines already that it's better to let the felucca pass a little further out, over here, yes, over there; then what should it go and do but hit the Breton rocks! It's wrecked, sinks, and Agilulf and Gurduloo just manage to bear Sophronia in safety to the shore.

Sophronia is weary. Agilulf decides to put her for refuge in a cave and then together with his squire go to Charlemagne's camp and announce her virginity to be still intact and so also the legitimacy of his name. Now I'm marking the cave with a small cross at this point of the Breton coast so as to be able to find it again later. I can't think what this line is doing passing the same place; by now my paper is such a mess of lines going in all directions. Ah yes, here's a line corresponding to Torrismund's journey. So the thought-laden youth is passing right here, while Sophronia lies in the cave. He too approaches the cave, enters, sees her.

{ 10 }

HOW had Torrismund got there? While Agilulf was moving from France to England, England to Africa, and Africa to Brittany, the putative cadet of the House of Cornwall had wandered far and wide over forests of Christian lands in search of the secret camp of the Knights of the Holy Grail. As the Holy Order has a habit of changing its headquarters from year to year, and never makes a show of its presence to the profane, Torrismund could find no indications to follow in his journey. He wandered about at random, chasing a remote sensation which was the same for him as the name of the Grail. But was it the order of the pious Knights he was searching for, or the memory of his childhood on Scottish heaths? Sometimes the sudden opening of a valley black with larches, or a cleft of grey rocks at the end of which boomed a torrent white with spray, filled him with an inexplicable emotion which he took for a warning. "Perhaps they're here, nearby." And if from nearby rose the faint and distant sound of a hunting horn then Torrismund lost all doubts, and began searching every crevice yard by yard for trace of them. But at most he would run into some lost huntsman or shepherd with his flock.

On reaching the remote land of Koowalden, he stopped in a village and asked the local rustics to be so good as to give him some goat's cheese and black bread.

"Willingly would we give you some, sir," said a goatherd, "but see how I, my wife and children are reduced to skeletons! We have to make so many offerings to the knights! This wood is crawling with colleagues of yours, though differently dressed. There's a whole troop of 'em, and for supplies, you know, they all come down on us!"

"Knights living in the wood? How are they dressed?"

"In white cloaks and golden helmets with two white swans' wings on the sides."

"Are they very holy?"

"Oh, yes they're holy enough. And they certainly never soil their hands with money, as they haven't a cent. But they expect a lot and we have to obey. Now we're stripped clean, and there's a famine. What shall we give them when they come next time?"

But the young man was already hurrying towards the wood.

Amid the fields, on the calm waters of a brook, slowly passed a flock of swans. Torrismund followed them along the bank. From among the bushes resounded an arpeggio, "Flin, flin, flin!" The youth walked on and the sound seemed at times to be following him and at others preceding him, "Flin, flin, flin!" Where the bushes thinned out appeared a human figure. It was a warrior in a helmet decorated with white wings, carrying both a lance and a small harp on which now and again he struck that chord, "Flin, flin, flin!" He said nothing. His eyes did not avoid Torrismund but passed over him as if not perceiving him, although they seemed to be following him. When tree trunks and branches separated them, the warrior led Torrismund onto the right track by calling with one of his arpeggios, "Flin, flin, flin!" Torrismund longed to talk to him, ask him questions, but instead followed, silent and intimidated.

They came into a clearing. On every side were warriors armed with lances, in golden cuirasses, wrapped in long white cloaks, motionless, each turned in a different direction with his eyes staring into a void. One was feeding a swan with grains of corn, his eyes turned elsewhere. At a new arpeggio from the player, a warrior on horseback answered by raising his horn and sending out a long call. When he was silent all the warriors moved; each made a few steps in his direction and stopped again.

"Knights . . ." Torrismund plucked up courage to say, "excuse me, I may be mistaken, but are you not the Knights of the Grai——"

"Never pronounce the name!" interrupted a voice behind him. A knight with white hair had halted near him. "Is it not enough for you to come disturbing our holy recollection?"

"Oh do forgive me." The youth turned to him.

"I'm so happy to be among you! If you knew how long I've looked for you!"

"Why?"

"Why . . . ?" and his longing to proclaim his secret was stronger than his fear of committing sacrilege. "Because I'm your son!"

The old knight remained impassive. "Here neither fathers nor sons are acknowledged," said he after a moment of silence. "Whoever enters the Sacred Order leaves behind him all earthly relationships."

Torrismund felt more disappointed than repudiated. He would have preferred an angry reply from his chaste fathers, which he could have contradicted or argued with by giving proofs and invoking their common blood, but this calm reply, which did not deny the possibility of the facts but excluded all discussion on a matter of principle, was discouraging.

"My sole other aspiration is to be recognized as a son of the Sacred Order," he tried to insist, "for which I bear a limitless admiration."

"If you admire our Order so much," said the old man, "you should have one sole aspiration, to be admitted as part of it."

"Would that be possible, d'you think?" exclaimed Torrismund, immediately attracted by the new pospect.

"When you have made yourself worthy."

"What must one do?"

"Purify oneself gradually from every passion and let oneself be possessed by love of the Grail."

"Oh, you *do* pronounce that name then?"

"We knights can; you profane, no."

"But tell me, why are all here silent and you the only one to talk?"

"I am charged with the duty of relations with the profane. Words being often impure, the Knights prefer to abstain from them, and also to let the Grail speak through their lips."

"Tell me what must I do to begin?"

"D'you see that maple leaf? A drop of dew has formed on it. Try and stand quite still and stare at the drop on that leaf, identify yourself with it, forget all the world in that drop, until you feel you have lost yourself and are pervaded by the infinite strength of the Grail."

And he left him. Torrismund stared fixedly at the drop, stared and stared, began thinking of his own affairs, saw a frog jumping on the leaf, stared and stared at the frog, and then at the drop again, moved a foot which had gone numb, and then suddenly felt bored. In the woods knights appeared and disappeared, moving very slowly, their mouths open and eyes staring, accompanied by swans whose soft plumage they caressed every now and again. One suddenly threw wide his arms and with a hoarse cry broke into a little run.

"That one over there," Torrismund could not prevent himself from asking the old man, who had reappeared nearby, "what's up with him?"

"Ecstasy!" said the old man. "That is something you will never know, who are so distracted and curious. Those brothers have finally reached complete communion with the all."

"And what about those?" asked the youth. Some knights were swaying about as if taken by slight shivers, and yawning.

"They're still at an intermediate stage. Before feeling one with the sun and stars the novice feels as if he has the nearest objects within himself, very intensely. This has an effect, particularly on the youngest. Those brothers of ours whom you see are feeling a pleasant gentle tickle from the running brook, the rustling leaves, the mushrooms growing underground."

"And don't they tire of it in the long run?"

"Gradually they reach the higher states in which the nearest vibrations no longer occupy them but the great sweep of the skies, and very slowly they detach themselves from the senses."

"Does that happen to all?"

"To few. And completely, only to one of us, the Elect, the King of the Grail."

They had reached a glade where a large number of knights were exercising their arms before a canopied tribunal. Under that canopy was sitting or rather crouching, motionless, someone who seemed to be more mummy than man, dressed too in the uniform of the Grail, but more sumptuously. His eyes were open, indeed staring, in a face dried up as a chestnut.

"Is he alive?" asked the youth.

"He's alive, but now he's so rapt by love of the Grail that he no longer needs to eat or move or do his

daily needs, or scarcely to breathe. He neither feels nor
sees. No one knows his thoughts; they certainly reflect the movements of distant planets."

"But why do they make him preside over military
parades, if he doesn't see?"

" 'Tis a rite of the Grail."

The knights were fencing among themselves.
They were moving their swords in jerks, looking into the
void, and taking sharp sudden steps as if they could
never foresee what they would do a second later.
And yet they never missed a blow.

"How can they fight with that air of being half
asleep?"

" 'Tis the Grail in us moving our swords. Love of
the universe can take the form of great frenzy and
urge us lovingly to pierce our enemies. Our Order is
invincible in war just because we fight without making
any effort or choice but letting the sacred frenzy flow
through our bodies."

"And does it always turn out all right?"

"Yes, with whoever has lost all residues of human
will and only lets the Grail direct his slightest gesture."

"Slightest gesture? Even now when you're walking?"

The old man was walking like a somnambulist.
"Certainly. It's not I who am moving my feet. I am
letting them be moved. Try. 'Tis the start of all."

Torrismund tried, but first he just could not succeed, and secondly he did not enjoy it. There were
the woods, green and leafy, all fluttering and achirp,
where he longed to run and let himself go and put

up game, to pit himself, his strength, his effort, his courage against that shadow, that mystery, that extraneous nature. Instead of which he had to stand there swaying like a paralytic.

"Let yourself be possessed," the old man was warning him, "let yourself be possessed entirely."

"But really, you know," burst out Torrismund, "what I long for is to possess, not be possessed."

The old man crossed his elbows over his face so as to stop up eyes and ears. "You still have a long way to go, my boy."

Torrismund remained in the encampment of the Grail. He tried hard to learn and imitate his fathers or brothers (he didn't know which to call them), tried to suffocate every motion of the mind which seemed too individual, to fuse himself in communion with the infinite love of the Grail, attentive for any indication of those ineffable sensations which sent the knights into ecstasies. But days passed and his purification made no progress. Everything they most liked bored him utterly: those voices, that music, their constant aptness to vibrate. And above all the continual proximity of the brethren, dressed like that, half naked, with golden breastplates and helmets, and very white flesh, some old, others fussy, touchy youths, all became more and more antipathetic to him. With their story about the Grail always moving them, they indulged in all sorts of loose habits while pretending to be ever pure.

The thought that he could have been generated like that, by people with eyes staring into the void without even thinking of what they were doing, forgetting right away, he found quite unbearable.

The day came for handing over tribute. All the villagers around the wood, in carefully arranged order, were to hand over to the Knights of the Grail a certain number of goats' cheeses, baskets of carrots, sacks of millet and young lambs.

A delegation of peasants advanced. "We wish to put forward the fact that the year has been a very bad one over the whole land of Koowalden. We are at our wits' end even to feed our children. Famine touches rich and poor. Pious Knights, we have come humbly to ask you to forgo our tribute just this time."

The King of the Grail, under the canopy, sat silent and still as ever. But at a certain moment, slowly, he unjoined his hands, which he had crossed over his stomach, raised them to the sky (he had very long nails), and from his mouth came, "Iiiih . . ."

At that sound all the Knights advanced with set lances towards the poor peasants. "Help! Let's defend ourselves!" they cried. "We'll hurry off and arm ourselves with axes and pitchforks!" and they dispersed.

The Knights, their eyes turned to the sky, marched to the sound of horns and timbrels. From hop rows and bushes leapt villagers armed with pitchforks and billhooks, trying to contest their passage. But they could do little against the Knights' inexorable lances. Breaking their scattered defenses, the knights flung their heavy chargers against the huts of stone and straw and mud, grinding them under hooves, deaf to the shout of women, calves, children. Other Knights bore lit torches and set fire to roofs, haystacks, stalls and a few poor granaries, until the villages were reduced to crackling bonfires.

Torrismund, in the wake of the Knights, was horrified.

"Why, tell me, why?" he cried to the old man, keeping behind him as the only one who could listen to him. "So it's not true you are pervaded by love of all! Hey, be careful, you're running down that old woman! How have you the hearts to attack these poor folk? Help, the flames are licking that cradle! What're you doing?"

"Do not scrutinize the designs of the Grail, novice!" warned the old man. "We are here but for this: 'tis the Grail moving us! Abandon yourself to its burning love."

But Torrismund had dismounted, rushed to the help of a mother and gave her back a fallen baby.

"No! Don't take my crop! I've worked so hard for it!" yelled an old man.

Torrismund was beside him. "Drop that sack, you brigand!" and he rushed at a Knight and tore the bag from him.

"Blessings on you! Stay with us!" cried some of the poor wretches, trying with pitchforks and knives to defend themselves behind a wall.

"Get into a semicircle, and we'll attack 'em together," shouted Torrismund at them, and so put himself at the head of the local militia.

Now he ejected the Knights from the houses. At

one moment he found himself face to face with the old Knight and another two armed with torches. "He's a traitor, take him!"

A fierce struggle rose. The locals used spits, and their women and children stones. Suddenly a horn sounded "Retreat!" Before the peasant counterattack the Knights had fallen back at many points and were now clearing out of the village.

The group pressing Torrismund hard retired too. "Away brothers!" shouted the old man. "Let us be led where the Grail takes us."

"The Grail will triumph," chorused the others, turning their bridles.

"Hurrah! You've saved us!" The peasants crowded round Torrismund. "You're a knight, but you're generous! At last one who is! Stay with us! Tell us what you want; we'll give it to you."

"Well . . . what I want . . . Now I don't know," stuttered Torrismund.

"We knew nothing either, even if we were human, before this battle . . And now we seem to be able . . . to want . . . to need to do things . . . however difficult . . ." and they turned to mourn their dead.

"I can't stay with you . . . I don't know who I am . . . Farewell!" and away he galloped.

"Come back!" cried the peasants, but Torrismund was already far from the village, from the wood of the Grail, from Koowalden.

Again he began his wandering among nations. Till now he had despised every honor and pleasure, his sole ideal being the Sacred Order of the Knights of the Grail. And now that ideal had vanished. To what aim could he set his disquiet?

He fed on wild fruit in the woods, on bean soup in monasteries he found on the way, on shellfish along rocky coasts. And on the shores of Brittany, seeking for shellfish in a cave, what should he find but a sleeping woman.

The restlessness which had moved him over the world, to places of soft velvety vegetation swept by low searing wind, into tense sunless days, now, at the sight of those long black lashes lowered over full pale cheeks, and that tender relaxed body, and the hand on the full-formed bosom, the soft loose hair, the lip, the hip, the toe, the breath, finally seemed assuaged.

He was leaning over her, looking, when Sophronia opened her eyes. "You'll do me no harm," she said gently, "what do you seek for amid these deserted rocks?"

"I seek something which I have always lacked and only now that I see you do I know what it is. How did you reach this shore?"

"Though a nun, I was forced to marry a follower of Mohammed but the nuptials were never consummated as I was the three hundred and sixty-fifth wife and Christian arms intervened. Because I was a victim of ferocious pirates and was forced to abandon ship, I was brought here."

"I understand. And are you alone?"

"My deliverer has gone to the Imperial camp to make certain arrangements, as far as I understand."

"I yearn to offer the protection of my sword, but

fear that the emotion firing me at sight of you may turn to suggestions which you might not consider honest."

"Oh, have no scruples, you know, I've seen so much. Though every time, just at the very moment, arrives that deliverer, always the same one."

"Will he arrive this time too?"

"Oh well, one never knows."

"What is your name?"

"Azira or Sister Palmyra according to whether I'm in a Sultan's harem or a convent."

"Azira, I seem always to have loved you . . . already to have lost myself in you . . ."

{ II }

CHARLEMAGNE was prancing along towards the coast of Brittany. "We'll soon see, we'll soon see, Agilulf of the Guildivern, calm yourself. If what you tell me is true, if this woman still bears the same virginity as she had fifteen years ago, then there's no more to be said, and you have been an armed knight by full right, and that young man was just trying to deceive us. To make certain I have brought along in our suite an old woman who's an expert in such matters. We soldiers haven't quite got the touch for these things, eh . . ."

The old midwife, on the crupper of Gurduloo's saddle, was twittering away, "Yes, yes, Majesty, I'll be most careful, even if it's twins . . ." She was deaf and had not yet understood what it was all about.

Into the grotto first went two officers of the suite, bearing torches. They returned in some confusion. "Sire, the virgin is lying in the embrace of a young soldier."

The lovers were brought before the emperor.

"You, Sophronia!" cried Agilulf.

Charlemagne had the young man's face raised. "Torrismund!"

Torrismund started towards Sophronia. "Are you Sophronia? Ah, my own mother!"

"Do you know this young man, Sophronia?" asked the emperor.

The woman bent her head, pale-faced, "If it's Torrismund, I brought him up myself," said she in a faint voice.

Torrismund leapt into his saddle. "I've committed foul incest! Never will you see me more!" He spurred and galloped off into the woods to the right.

Agilulf spurred off in his turn. "Nor will you see me again!" said he. "I have no longer a name! Farewell!" And he rode off deep into the woods on the left.

All remained in consternation. Sophronia hid her head between her hands.

Suddenly came a thud of hooves from the right. It was Torrismund galloping back out of the wood at full tilt. He shouted, "Hey! She was a virgin until a short time ago! Why didn't I think of that at once? She was a virgin! She can't be my mother!"

"Would you explain?" asked Charlemagne.

"In truth, Torrismund is not my son, but my brother or rather half-brother," said Sophronia. "Our mother the Queen of Scotland—my father the King having been at the wars for a year—bore him after a chance encounter, it seems, with the Sacred Order of the Knights of the Grail. When the king announced his return, that perfidious woman (as am I forced to

consider our mother) with the excuse of my taking
my little brother for a walk, let us loose in the
woods. And she arranged a foul deceit for her husband
on his arrival. She said that I, then aged thirteen,
had run away to bear a little bastard. Held back by
ill-conceived respect, I never betrayed our mother's
secret. I lived on the heaths with my infant half-
brother, and they were free and happy years for me,
compared with those awaiting me in the convent which
I was forced to enter by the Duke of Cornwall. Never
until this morning at the age of thirty-three have I
known man, and my first experience turns out to be
incestuous..."

"Let's think it all over calmly," said Charlemagne, conciliatingly. "It is incest, of course, but
that between half-brother and sister is not the most
serious."

"'Tis not incest, Sacred Majesty! Rejoice,
Sophronia!" exclaimed Torrismund, radiant. "In my
researches on my origin I learnt a secret which I
wished to keep forever. She whom I thought my
mother, that is you, Sophronia, was not born of the
Queen of Scotland but is the King's natural daughter
by a farmer's wife. The King had you adopted by his
wife, that is, by her who I now learn from you was
my mother and your stepmother. Now I understand
how she, obliged by the king to pretend herself your
mother against her wish, longed for a chance to be
rid of you and she did so by attributing to you the
result of a passing adventure of her own, myself. You
are the daughter of the King of Scotland and of a peasant woman, I of the Queen and of the Sacred Order;

we have no blood tie, only the link of love forged freely here a short time ago and which I ardently hope you will be willing to reforge."

"All seems to be working out for the best . . ." said Charlemagne, rubbing his hands. "Let us hasten to trace our fine knight Agilulf and reassure him that his name and title are no longer in danger."

"I will go myself, Majesty!" cried a knight, running forward. It was Raimbaut.

He entered the woods, shouting, "Knight! Sir Agilulf! Knight of the Guildivern, . . . Agilulf Emo Bertrandin of the Guildivern and of the Others of Corbentraz and Sura, Knight of Selimpia Citeriore and Feeeez! . . . All's in oooorder! . . . Come baaack!"

Only the echo replied.

Raimbaut began to search the woods track by track, and off the tracks over crags and torrents, calling, ears stretched, seeking a sign, a trace. He saw the marks of horse's hooves. At a certain point they were stamped deeper, as if the animal had stopped. From there on the trail of hooves grew lighter, as if the horse had been let loose. But at the same point diverged another trail, a trail of iron footsteps. Raimbaut followed that.

On reaching a clearing he held his breath. At the foot of an oak tree, scattered over the ground, were an overturned helmet with a crest of iridescent plumes, a white breastplate, greaves, arm pieces, basinet, gauntlets, in fact all the pieces of Agilulf's armor, some disposed as if in an attempt at an ordered pyramid, others rolled haphazardly on the ground. On the hilt of the sword was a note, "I leave this armor to Sir Raimbaut of Roussillon." Beneath was a half squiggle, as of a signature begun and interrupted.

"Knight!" called Raimbaut, turning towards the helmet, the breastplate, the oak tree, the sky. "Knight! Take back your armor! Your rank in the army and the nobility of France is assured!" and he tried to put the armor together, to stand it on its feet, continuing to shout, "You're all set, sir, no one can deny it now!" No voice replied. The armor would not stand. The helmet rolled on the ground. "Knight, you have resisted so long by your will power alone, and succeeded in doing all things as if you existed, why suddenly surrender?" But he did not know in which direction to turn; the armor was empty, not empty like before, but empty of that something going by the name of Sir Agilulf which was now dissolved like a drop in the sea.

Raimbaut then unstrapped his own armor, stripped, put on the white armor, donned Agilulf's helmet, grasped his shield and sword, leapt on his horse. Thus accouterd he appeared before the emperor and his retinue.

"Ah, Agilulf, so you're back, are you, and all's settled, eh?"

But another voice replied from the helmet. "I'm not Agilulf, Majesty!" The visor was raised and Raimbaut's face appeared. "All that remains of the Knight of the Guildivern is his white armor and this paper assigning me its possession. Now my one longing is to fling myself into battle!"

The trumpets sounded the alarm. A fleet of feluccas had just landed a Saracen host in Brittany. The Frankish army hurried to arms. "Your desire is granted!" cried Charlemagne. "Now is the hour of battle. Do honor to the arms you bear! Although Agilulf had a difficult character, he was a fine soldier."

The Frankish army held the invaders at bay, opened a breach in the Saracen ranks through which young Raimbaut was the first to rush. He lay about him, giving blows and taking them. Many a Moor bit the dust. On Raimbaut's lance were spitted as many as it could take. Already the invading hordes were falling back on their moored feluccas. Hard pressed by Frankish arms, the defeated invaders took off from shore, except those who remained to soak the grey Breton soil with Moorish blood.

Raimbaut issued from battle victorious and untorched, but his armor, Agilulf's impeccable white armor, was now all encrusted with earth, bespattered with enemy blood, covered with dents, scratches and slashes, the helmet askew, the shield gashed in the very midst of that mysterious coat of arms. Now the youth felt it to be truly his own armor, his, Raimbaut of Roussillon's. His first discomfort on donning it was gone; now it fitted him like a glove.

He was galloping, all alone, on the edge of a hill. A voice rang from the bottom of the valley, "Hey, up there! Agilulf!"

A knight was coursing towards him, in armor covered with a mantle of periwinkle blue. It was Bradamante following him. "At last I've found you, white knight!"

"Bradamante, I'm not Agilulf, I'm Raimbaut!" he was on the point of calling in reply, but thought it better to say so from nearby, and turned his horse to reach her.

"At last 'tis you coursing to meet me, oh unseizable warrior!" exclaimed Bradamante. "Oh, that it should be granted me to see you rushing so after me, you the only man whose actions are not mere impulse, shallow caprice, like those of the usual rabble who follow me!" And so saying, she wheeled her horse and tried to escape him, though turning her head every now and again to see if he were playing her game and following her.

Raimbaut was impatient to say to her, "Don't you notice how I too move awkwardly, how my every gesture betrays desire, dissatisfaction, disquiet? All I wish is to be one who knows what he wants!" And to tell her so he galloped after her, as she laughed and called, "This is the day I've always dreamt of!"

He lost sight of her. There was a grassy solitary vale. Her horse was tied to a mulberry tree. It was like that first time he had followed her when still not suspecting her to be a woman. Raimbaut dismounted. There she was, lying down on a mossy slope. She had taken off her armor, was dressed in a short topaz-colored tunic. As she lay there she opened her arms to him. Raimbaut went forward in his white armor. This was the moment to say, "I'm not Agilulf. The armor with which you fell in love is now filled out with the weight of a body, a young agile one like mine. Don't you see how this armor has lost its inhuman whiteness and become a covering for battle, which

is exposed to every blow, a tool, patient and useful?"
This was what he wanted to say, instead of which he
stood there with trembling hands, taking hesitant
steps towards her. Perhaps the best thing would be
to show himself, to take off his armor, make it clear
that he is Raimbaut, particularly now as she closes
her eyes and lies there with a smile of expectation.
Tensely the young man tore off his armor; now
Bradamante would open her eyes and recognize him
. . . No; she had put a hand over her face as if not
wanting to be disturbed by the sight of the nonexistent knight's invisible approach, and Raimbaut
flung himself on her.

"Yes, I was sure of it!" exclaimed Bradamante,
with closed eyes. "I was always sure it would be possible!" and she hugged him close, and in a fever of
which both partook, they were united. "Yes, oh yes,
I was sure of it!"

Now it's over and the moment comes to look
each other in the eyes.

"She'll see me," Raimbaut thinks in a flash
of pride and hope. "She'll understand all. She'll understand it's been right and fine and love me for ever!"

Bradamante opens her eyes.

"You!"

She leaps from her couch, pushes Raimbaut back.

"You! You!" she cries, her mouth enraged, her
eyes starting with tears. "You! Impostor!"

And on foot she brandishes her sword, raises it
against Raimbaut and hits him, but with the flat, on
his head, stuns him, and all he can bring out as he
raises unarmed hands to defend himself or embrace

her is, "But, but . . . tell me . . . wasn't it good . . . ?"
Then he loses his senses and hears only vaguely the
clatter of her departing horse.

If a lover is wretched who invokes kisses of which
he knows not the flavor, a thousand times more
wretched is he who has had a taste of the flavor and
then had it denied him. Raimbaut continued his intrepid warrior's life. Wherever the fight was thickest,
there his lance cleft. If in the turmoil of swords he
spied a glint of periwinkle blue, he would rush towards it. "Bradamante!" he would shout, but always
in vain.

The only person to whom he wanted to confess
his troubles had vanished. Sometimes, in his wandering
around the bivouacs, the way some armor stood erect
on its side pieces made him quiver, for it reminded
him of Agilulf. Suppose the Knight had not dissolved
but found some other armor? Raimbaut would go up
and say, "Don't think me offensive, colleague, but
would you mind raising the visor of your helmet?"

Every time he hoped to find himself facing an
emptiness, instead of which there was always a nose
above a pair of twisted moustaches. "I'm sorry," he
would murmur, and turn away.

Another was also searching for Agilulf: Gurduloo,
who every time he saw an empty pot, cauldron or
tub would stop and exclaim, "Oh *sor* master! At your
orders, *sor* master."

Sitting in a field on the verge of a road, he was
making a long speech into the mouth of a wine
flask when a voice interrupted him, "What are you
seeking inside there, Gurduloo?"

It was Torrismund, who, having celebrated his solemn nuptials with Sophronia in the presence of Charlemagne, was riding off with his bride and a rich suite to Koowalden, of which the emperor had named him Count.

"It's my master I'm looking for," says Gurduloo.

"In that flask?"

"My master is a person who doesn't exist, so he can not exist as much in a flask as in a suit of armor."

"But your master has dissolved into thin air!"

"Then am I squire to the air?"

"You will be my squire, if you follow me."

They reached Koowalden. The country was unrecognizable. Instead of villages now rose towns and houses of stone, and mills, and canals.

"I have returned, good folk, to stay among you . . ."

"Hurrah! Fine! Hurrah! Long live the bride!"

"Wait and show your joy at the news I bring you. The Emperor Charlemagne—bow to his sacred name—has invested me with the title of Count of Koowalden."

"Ah . . . But . . . Charlemagne? . . . Well . . ."

"Don't you understand? You have a Count now! I will defend you against the incursions of the Knights of the Grail."

"Oh we've thrust all those out of the whole of Koowalden some time ago! You see, we've always obeyed for so long . . . But now we've seen one can live quite well without having truck with either knights or counts . . . We cultivate the land, have put up artisan shops and mills, and try to get our laws respected by ourselves, to defend our borders, in fact we're moving ahead and not complaining. You're a generous young man and we'll not forget what you've done for us . . . Stay here if you wish . . . but as equals . . ."

"As equals? You don't want me as Count? But don't you understand it's the emperor's order? It's impossible for you to refuse!"

"Oh, people are always saying that! Impossible! . . . To get rid of those Grail people seemed impossible . . . and then we only had pitchforks and billhooks . . . We wish no ill to anyone, young sir, and to you least of all . . . You're a fine young man, and know many things which we don't . . . If you stay here as equals with us and do no bullying, maybe you will become the first among us just the same . . ."

"Torrismund, I am weary of so many mishaps," said Sophronia, raising her veil. "These good people seem reasonable and courteous and the town pleasanter and in better state than many . . . Why should we not try to come to an arrangement?"

"What about our suite?"

"They can all become citizens of Koowalden," replied the inhabitants, "and to each will be given according to his worth."

"Am I to consider myself an equal to this squire of mine, Gurduloo, who doesn't even know if he exists or not?"

"He will learn too . . . We ourselves did not know we existed . . . One can also learn to be . . ."

{ 12 }

BOOK, now you have reached your end. These last
pages I found myself writing away at breakneck speed.
From one line to another I have leapt about among
nations and seas and continents. What is this frenzy
which has seized me, this impatience? It's as if I
were waiting for something. But what can nuns await,
withdrawn here so as to be outside the ever-changing
happenings of the world? What else can I await except new pages to cover and the routine ringing of the
convent bells?

There, I hear a horse come up the narrow track.
Now it stops right at the convent gates. The rider
knocks. I can't stretch far enough out of my little window to see him, but I can hear his voice. "Hey, good
sisters, listen!"

But is that his voice, or am I mistaken? Yes, 'tis
Raimbaut's voice which I have so long made resound
over these pages! What can Raimbaut want here?

"Hey, good sisters, can you please tell me if an
Amazon has found refuge in this convent, the famous
Bradamante?"

Yes, searching for Bradamante throughout the world, Raimbaut was bound to reach here one day.

I hear the Sister Guardian's voice reply, "No, soldier, there are no Amazons here, only poor holy women praying for your sins."

But now I run to the window and cry, "Yes, Raimbaut, I'm here, wait for me, I knew you'd come, I'll be down, I'll leave with you."

And hurriedly I tear off my cloistral bands, my nun's skirt, pull out of a drawer my little topaz-colored tunic, my cuirass, my helmet, my spurs, my periwinkle blue robe. "Wait for me, Raimbaut, I'm here, I'm here, I, Bradamante!"

Yes, my book. Sister Theodora who tells this tale and the Amazon Bradamante are one and the same. Sometimes I gallop over battlefields after adventures of duels and loves, sometimes I shut myself in convents, meditating and jotting down the adventures that have happened to me, so as to try and understand them. When I came to shut myself in here I was desperate with love for Agilulf, now I burn for the young and passionate Raimbaut.

That is why my pen at a certain point began running on so. I rush to meet him. I knew he would not be long in coming. A page is good only when we turn it and find life urging along, confusing every page in the book. The pen rushes on, urged by the same joy that makes me course the open road. A chapter started when one doesn't know which tale to tell is like a corner turned on leaving a convent, when one might come face to face with a dragon, a Saracen gang, an enchanted isle or a new love.

I'm hurrying to you, Raimbaut. I'm not even bidding the abbess good-bye. They know me already and know that after affrays and affairs and blighted hopes I always return to this cloister. But it will be different now . . . It will be . . .

From describing the past, from the present which seized my hand in its excited grasp, here I am, O future, now mounting the crupper of your horse. What new pennants wilt thou unfurl before me from towers of cities not yet founded? What rivers of devastation set flowing over castles and gardens I have loved? What unforeseeable golden ages art thou preparing—ill-mastered, indomitable harbinger of treasures dearly paid for, my kingdom to be conquered, the future . . .

THE END

The
CLOVEN
Viscount

{ I }

THERE was a war on against the Turks. My uncle, the Viscount Medardo of Terralba, was riding towards the Christian camp across the plain of Bohemia, followed by a squire called Kurt. Storks were flying low, in white flocks, through the thick, still air.

"Why all the storks?" Medardo asked Kurt. "Where are they flying?"

My uncle was a new arrival, just enrolled to please ducal neighbors involved in that war. After fitting himself out with a horse and squire at the last castle in Christian hands, he was now on his way to report at Imperial headquarters.

"They're flying to the battlefields," said the squire glumly. "They'll be with us all the way."

The Viscount Medardo had heard that in those parts a flight of storks was thought a good omen, and he wanted to seem pleased at the sight. But in spite of himself he felt worried.

"What can draw such birds to a battlefield, Kurt?" he asked.

"They eat human flesh too, nowadays," replied

the squire, "since the fields have been stripped by famine and the rivers dried by drought. Vultures and crows have now given way to storks and flamingos and cranes."

My uncle was then in his first youth, the age in which confused feelings, not yet sifted, all rush into good and bad, the age in which every new experience, even macabre and inhuman, is palpitating and warm with love of life.

"What about the crows then? And the vultures?" he said. "And the other birds of prey? Where have they gone?" He was pale, but his eyes glittered.

The squire, a dark-skinned soldier with a heavy moustache, never raised his eyes. "They ate so many plague-ridden bodies, the plague got 'em too," and he pointed his lance at some black bushes, which a closer look revealed were not made of branches, but of feathers and dried claws from birds of prey.

"One can't tell which died first, bird or man, or who tore the other to bits," said Kurt.

To escape the plague exterminating the population, entire families had taken to the open country, where death caught them. Over the bare plain were scattered tangled heaps of men's and women's corpses, naked, covered with plague boils, and, inexplicably at first, with feathers, as if those skinny legs and ribs had grown black feathers and wings. These were carcasses of vultures mingled with human remains.

The ground was now scattered with signs of past battles. Their progress slowed, for the two horses kept jibbing and rearing.

"What's the matter with our horses?" Medardo asked the squire.

"Signore," he replied, "horses hate nothing more than the stink of their own guts."

The patch of plain they were crossing was covered with horses' carcasses, some supine with hooves to the sky, others prone with muzzles dug into the earth.

"Why all these fallen horses round here, Kurt?" asked Medardo.

"When a horse feels its belly ripped open," explained the squire, "it tries to keep its guts in. Some put bellies on the ground, others turn on their backs to prevent them from dangling. But death soon gets 'em all the same."

"So mostly horses die in this war?"

"Turkish scimitars seem made to cleave their bellies at a stroke. Further on we'll see men's bodies. First it's horses, then riders. But there's the camp."

On the edge of the horizon rose the pinnacles of the highest tents, and the standards of the Imperial army, and smoke.

As they galloped on, they saw that those fallen in the last battle had nearly all been taken away and buried. There were just a few limbs, fingers in particular, scattered over the stubble.

"Every now and again I see a finger pointing our way," said my uncle Medardo. "What does that mean?"

"May God forgive them, but the living chop off the fingers of the dead to get at their rings."

"Who goes there?" said a sentinel in a cloak covered with mould and moss, like a tree bark exposed to the north wind.

"Hurrah for the Holy Imperial crown!" cried Kurt.

"And down with the Sultan!" replied the sentinel. "Please, though, when you get to headquarters, do ask 'em to send along my relief, because I'm starting to grow roots!"

The horses were now at a gallop to escape the clouds of flies surrounding the camp and buzzing over heaps of excrement.

"Many's the brave man," observed Kurt, "whose dung is still on the ground when he's already in heaven," and he crossed himself.

At the entrance they rode past a series of canopies, beneath which thick-set women with long brocade gowns and bare breasts greeted them with yells and coarse laughter.

"The pavilions of the courtesans," said Kurt. "No other army has such fine women."

My uncle was riding with his head turned back to look at them.

"Careful, Signore," added the squire, "they're so foul and pox-ridden even the Turks wouldn't want them as booty. They're not only covered with lice, bugs and ticks, but even scorpions and lizards make their nests on them now."

They passed by the field batteries. At night the artillerymen cooked their ration of turnips and water on the bronze parts of swivel guns and cannons. burning hot from the day's firing.

Carts were arriving, full of earth, which the artillerymen were passing through sieves.

"Gunpowder is scarce now," explained Kurt, "but the soil of the battlefields is so saturated with it that a few charges can be retrieved there."

Next came the cavalry stables where, amid flies, the veterinarians were at work patching up hides with stitches, belts and plasters of boiling tar, while horses and doctors neighed and stamped.

The long stretches of infantry encampments followed. It was dusk, and in front of every tent soldiers were sitting with bare feet in tubs of warm water. As they were used to sudden alarms night and day, they kept helmet on head and pike tight in fist even at foot-bath time. Inside taller tents draped like kiosks, officers could be seen powdering armpits and waving lace fans.

"That's not from effeminacy," said Kurt, "just the opposite. They want to show how they're at ease in the rigors of military life."

The Viscount of Terralba was immediately introduced into the presence of the Emperor. In his pavilion, amid tapestries and trophies, the sovereign was studying future battle plans. Tables were covered with unrolled maps and the Emperor was busy sticking pins in them, taking these from a small pincushion proferred by one of the marshals. By then the maps were so covered with pins that it was impossible to understand a thing, and to read them, pins had to be taken out and then put back. With all this pinning and unpinning, the Emperor and his marshals, to keep their hands free, all had pins between their lips and could only talk in grunts.

At the sight of the youth bowing before him, the sovereign let out a questioning grunt and then took the pins out of his mouth.

"A knight just arrived from Italy, Your Majesty," they introduced him. "The Viscount of Terralba, from one of the noblest families of Genoa."

"Let him be made lieutenant at once."

My uncle clicked spurs to attention, while the Emperor gave a regal sweep of the arm and all the maps folded in on themselves and rolled away.

Though tired, Medardo went to sleep late that night. He walked up and down near his tent and heard calls of sentries, neighs of horses and broken speech from soldiers in sleep. He gazed up at the stars of Bohemia, thought of his new rank, of the battle next day, of his distant home and of the rustling reeds in its brooks. He felt no nostalgia or doubt, or apprehension. Things were still indisputably whole as he was himself. Could he have foreseen the dreadful fate awaiting him, he might have even found it quite natural, with all its pain. His eyes kept straying towards the edge of the dark horizon where he knew the enemy camp lay, and he hugged himself with crossed arms, content to be certain both of the distant and differing reality, and of his own presence amidst it. He sensed the bloodshed in that cruel war, poured over the earth in innumerable streams, reaching even him, and he let it lap over him without feeling outrage or pity.

BATTLE began punctually at ten in the morning. From high on his saddle Lieutenant Medardo gazed over the broad array of Christians ready for attack, and raised his face to the wind of Bohemia, swirling with chaff like some dusty barn!

"No, don't turn round, Signore," exclaimed Kurt, now a sergeant, beside him. And to justify the peremptory phrase he murmured, "It's said to bring bad luck before battle."

In reality he did not want the Viscount to feel discouraged, for he knew that the Christian army consisted almost entirely of the line drawn up there, and that the only reinforcements were a few platoons of rickety infantry.

But my uncle was looking into the distance, at an approaching cloud on the horizon, and was thinking: "There, that cloud contains the Turks, the real Turks, and these men next to me, spitting tobacco, are veterans of Christendom, and this bugle now sounding is the attack, the first attack in my life, and this roaring and shaking, this shooting star plunging to

earth and treated with languid irritation by veterans
and horses is a cannon ball, the first enemy cannon
ball I've ever seen. May it not be the day when I'll
say—'And it's my last.'"

Then, with bared sword, he was galloping over
the plain, his eyes on the Imperial standard vanishing
and reappearing amid the smoke, while friendly cannon balls rotated in the sky above his head, and enemy
ones opened gaps in the Christian ranks and created
umbrellas of earth. "I'll see the Turks! I'll see the
Turks!" he was thinking. There's no greater fun than
having enemies and then finding out if they are like
one thought.

Now he saw them, saw the Turks. Two came right
up, on mantled horses. They had round little leather
shields, black and saffron striped robes, turbans, ocher-
colored faces and moustaches, like someone at Terralba called "Micky the Turk." One of the two was
killed and the other killed someone else. But now
numbers of them were arriving and the hand-to-hand
fighting began. To see two Turks was to see the lot.
They were soldiers, too, all in their own army equip-
ment. Their faces were tanned and tough, like peasants'. Medardo had seen as much as he wanted to of
them. He felt he might as well get back to Terralba
in time for the quail season. But he had signed on for
the whole war. So on he rushed, avoiding scimitar
thrusts, until he found a short Turk, on foot, and
killed him. Now that he had got the hang of it he
looked round for a tall one on horseback. That was
a mistake, for small ones were the most dangerous.

They got right under horses with those scimitars and hamstrung them.

Medardo's horse stopped short with legs splayed. "What's up?" said the Viscount. Kurt came up and pointed downwards. "Look there." All its guts were hanging to the ground. The poor beast looked up at its master, then lowered its head as if to browse on its intestines, but that was only a last show of heroism; it fainted, then died. Medardo of Terralba was on foot.

"Take my horse, Lieutenant," said Kurt, but did not manage to halt it, as he fell from the saddle, wounded by a Turkish arrow, and the horse ran away.

"Kurt!" cried the Viscount, and went to his squire, who was groaning on the ground.

"Don't think of me, sir," said the squire. "Let's hope there will be some schnapps in the hospital. A can is due to every wounded man."

My uncle Medardo flung himself into the melee. The fate of battle was uncertain. In the confusion it seemed the Christians were winning. They had certainly broken the Turkish lines and turned some of their positions. My uncle with other bold spirits even got close up to the enemy guns as the Turks moved them to keep the Christians under fire. Two of the Turkish artillerymen were pivoting a cannon. With their slow movements, beards, and long robes, they looked like a pair of astronomers. My uncle said, "I'll see to them." In his enthusiasm and inexperience he did not know that cannons are to be approached only by the side or the breech. He leapt in front of the muzzle, with sword bared, thinking

he would frighten the two astronomers. Instead of
which they fired a cannonade right in his chest.
Medardo of Terralba jumped into the air.

After dusk, when a truce came, two carts went
gathering Christian bodies on the battlefield. One
was for the wounded and the other for the dead. A
first choice was made on the spot. "I'll take this one,
you take that." When it looked as if something was
salvageable, they put the man on the wounded cart;
where there was nothing but bits and pieces they
went on the cart of the dead, for decent burial. Those
who hadn't even a body were left for the storks. In
the last few days, as losses were growing, orders had
been given to be liberal about wounded. So Medardo's
remains were considered those of a wounded man
and put on that cart.

The second choice was made in the hospital.
After battles the field hospital was an even ghastlier
sight than the battle itself. On the ground were long
rows of stretchers with poor wretches in them, and
all around swarmed doctors, clutching forceps, saws,
needles, amputated joints and balls of string. From
body to body then went, doing their very best to
bring every one back to life. A saw here, a stitch there,
leaks plugged, veins turned inside out like gloves and
put back with more string than blood inside, but
patched up and shut. When a patient died whatever
good bits he still had in him went to patching up

another, and so on. What caused most confusion were intestines; once unrolled they just couldn't be put back.

When the sheet was pulled away, there lay the Viscount's body, horribly mutilated. It not only lacked an arm and leg, but the whole thorax and abdomen between that arm and leg had been swept away by the direct hit. All that remained of the head was one eye, one ear, one cheek, half a nose, half a mouth, half a chin and half a forehead; the other half of the head was just not there. The long and short of it was that just half of him had been saved, the right part, which was perfectly preserved, without a scratch on it, except for that huge slash separating it from the left-hand part blown away.

How pleased the doctors were! "A fine case!" If he didn't die in the meantime they might even try to save him. And they gathered round while poor soldiers with an arrow in the arm died of blood poisoning. They sewed, kneaded, stuck; who knows what they were up to. The fact is that next day my uncle opened his only eye, his half mouth, dilated his single nostril and breathed. The strong Terralba constitution had pulled him through. Now he was alive and half a man.

{ 3 }

WHEN my uncle made his return to Terralba I was seven or eight years old. It was late, after dusk, in October. The sky was cloudy. During the day we had been working on the vintage, and over the vine rows we saw approaching, on the grey sea, the sails of a ship flying the Imperial flag. At every ship we saw then we used to say, "There's Master Medardo back," not because we were impatient for his return, but in order to have something to wait for. This time we guessed right; and that evening we were sure, when a youth called Fiorfiero, who was pounding at the grapes on top of the vat, cried, "Ah, look down there!" It was almost dark and down in the valley we saw a row of torches being lit on the mule path. Then when the procession passed the bridge we made out a litter borne by hand. There was no doubt; it was the Viscount returning from the wars.

The news spread through the valley. People gathered in the castle courtyard: retainers, domestics, vintagers, shepherds, men at arms. The one person missing was Medardo's father, old Viscount Aiolfo, my grandfather, who had not been down to the courtyard for ages. Weary of worldly cares, he had renounced the privileges of his title in favor of his only son before the latter left for the wars. Now his passion for birds, which he raised in a huge aviary within the castle, was beginning to exclude all else. The old man had recently had his bed taken into the aviary too, and in there he shut himself, and didn't leave it night or day. His meals were handed through the grill of the cage together with the bird seed, which Aiolfo shared. And he spent his hours stroking pheasants and turtle doves, as he awaited his son's return.

Never had I seen so many people in the courtyard of our castle; gone were the days, which I'd only heard about, of feasts and neighbor's feuds. For the first time I realized how ravaged were the walls and towers, and how muddy the yard where we now foddered goats and filled troughs for pigs. As they waited, all were discussing in what state the Viscount Medardo would return. Rumors had reached us some time before of grave wounds inflicted by the Turks, but no one quite knew yet if he was mutilated or sick or only scored by scars. At the sight of the litter we prepared for the worst.

Now the litter was set on the ground, and from the blackness within came the glitter of a pupil. Sebastiana, his old nurse, made a move towards it, but from the dark came a raised hand with a sharp gesture of refusal. Then the body in the litter was seen to give angular and convulsive movements, and before our eyes Medardo of Terralba jumped to the ground, leaning on a crutch. A black cloak and hood covered him from head to foot; the right-hand part was thrown back, showing half his face and body close against the crutch, while on the left everything seemed hidden and wrapped in edges and folds of that ample drapery.

He stood looking at us, at the silent circle surrounding him, but maybe he was not looking at us out of that fixed eye at all, perhaps he just was lost in his own thoughts. A gust of wind blew from the sea and a broken branch on top of a fig tree groaned. My uncle's cloak waved, and the wind bellowed it out, stretched it taut like a sail. It almost seemed to be passing through the body as if that body was not there at all, and the cloak empty, like a ghost's. Then on looking closer we saw that it was clinging to him like a standard to its pole, and this pole was a shoulder, an arm, a side, a leg, all leaning on the crutch. The rest was not there at all.

Goats looked at the Viscount with fixed inexpressive stares, each from a different direction, but all tight against each other, their backs arranged in an odd pattern of right angles. Pigs, more sensitive and quick-witted, screamed and fled, bumping their flanks against each other. Even we could not hide our terror; "Oh my boy," cried old Sebastiana and raised her arms. "You poor little thing!"

My uncle, annoyed at making such an impression, advanced the point of his crutch on the ground and with a hop began pushing himself towards the castle entrance. But sitting cross-legged on the steps of the great gate were the litter bearers, half-naked men with gold earrings and crests and tufts of hair on shaven heads. They straightened up and one man with plaits who seemed their leader said, "We're waiting for our pay."

"How much?" asked Medardo, almost laughing.

The man with the plaits said, "You know the tariff for carrying a man in a litter . . ."

My uncle pulled a purse from his belt and threw it, tinkling, at the bearer's feet. The man quickly weighed it in a hand, and exclaimed, "But that's much less than we'd agreed on, Signore."

Medardo, as the wind raised the edges of his cloak, said, "Half."

He brushed past the litter bearer with little jumps on his single foot and went up the stairs, through the great open gate giving on to the interior of the castle, pushed his crutch at both the heavy doors which shut with a clang, and then as the wicket gate remained open banged that too and so vanished from our eyes. We continued to hear the alternating tap of foot and crutch from inside, moving down passages towards the wing of the castle where his private apartments lay, and also the banging and bolting of doors.

His father stood waiting behind the grill of the bird cage. Medardo had not even paused to greet him. He shut himself into his rooms alone, and refused to show himself or reply even to Sebastiana who knocked and sympathized for a long time.

Old Sebastiana was a big woman dressed in black

and veils, her red face without a wrinkle except for
one almost hiding her eyes. She had given milk to
all the males of the Terralba family, gone to bed with
all the older ones, and closed the eyes of all the dead
ones. Now she went to and fro between the apartments of the two self-imposed prisoners, not knowing
what to do to help them.

Next day, as Medardo gave no more sign of life,
we went back to our vintaging, but there was no
gaiety, and among the vines we talked of nothing but
his fate, not because we were so fond of him but
because the subject was fascinating and strange. Only
Sebastiana stayed in the castle, listening attentively
to every sound.

But old Aiolfo, as if foreseeing that his son would
return so glum and fierce, had already trained one of
his dearest birds, a shrike, to fly up to the castle wing
in which were Medardo's apartments, then empty,
and enter through the little window of his rooms.
That morning the old man opened the bird-cage door
to the shrike, followed its flight to his son's window,
then went back to scattering bird seed to magpies and
tits, and imitating their chirps.

A little later he heard the thud of something
flung against the windows. He leant out; there on the
pediment was the shrike, dead. The old man took it
up in the palms of his hands and saw that a wing was
broken off as if someone had tried to tear it, a claw
wrenched off as if by two fingers, and an eye gouged
out. The old man held the shrike tight to his breast
and began to sob.

That same day he took to his bed, and attendants on the other side of the cage saw that he was very ill. But no one could go and take care of him, as he had locked himself inside and hidden the keys. Birds flew around his bed. Since he had taken to it they had all refused to settle or stop fluttering their wings.

Next morning, when the nurse put her head into the bird cage, she realized that the Viscount Aiolfo was dead. The birds had all perched on his bed, as if it were a floating tree trunk in the midst of sea.

{ 4 }

AFTER his father's death Medardo began leaving the castle. Sebastiana was the first to notice when one morning she found his doors flung open and his rooms deserted. A group of servants was sent out through the countryside to follow the Viscount's path. The servants, hastening along, passed under a pear tree which they had seen the evening before loaded with tardy, still unripe, fruit. "Look up there," said one of the men; they stared at pears hanging against a whitish sky, and the sight filled them with terror. For the pears were not whole, but were cut in half, down the middle, and were still hanging on their own stalks. All there was of every pear was the right side (or left, according to which way one looked, but they were all on the same side) and the other half had vanished, cut or maybe eaten.

"The Viscount has passed by here!" said the servants.

Obviously, after being shut up without food for so long, he had felt hungry that night and climbed up the first tree he saw to eat pears.

As they went the servants met half a frog on a rock, still alive and jumping with the vitality of frogs. "We're on the right track!" and on they went. But they soon lost it, for they missed half a melon among the leaves, and had to turn back until they found it.

So they passed from fields to woods and saw a mushroom cut in half, an edible one, then another, a poisonous red *boletus*, and as they went deeper into the wood kept finding every now and again mushrooms sprouting from the ground on half a leg and with only half an umbrella. These seemed divided by a neat cut, and of the other half not even a spore was to be seen. They were fungi of all kinds, puff balls, ovules and toadstools—and as many were poisonous as eatable.

Following this scattered trail, the servants came to an open space called "The Nun's Field," with a pool in the middle of the grass. It was dawn and on the edge of the pool stood Medardo wrapped in his black cloak looking at his reflection in the water, on which floated white, yellow and dun-colored mushrooms. They were the halves of the mushrooms he had carried off, scattered now on that transparent surface. On the water the mushrooms looked whole, and the Viscount was gazing at them. The servants hid on the other side of the pool and did not dare say a thing, but just stared at the floating mushrooms, until suddenly they realized that those were the edible ones. Where were the poisonous ones? If he had not flung them into the pool, what could he have done with them? Back the servants set off through the woods at a run. They did not have to go far because on the path they met a child carrying a basket, and inside it were all the poisonous halves.

The child was myself. That night I had been playing alone around the Nun's Field giving myself frights by bursting out of trees, when I met my uncle hopping along by moonlight over the field on his one leg, with a basket on his arm.

"Hullo, uncle!" I shouted. It was the first time I was able to call him that.

He seemed vexed at the sight of me. "I'm out for mushrooms," he explained.

"And have you got any?"

"Look," said my uncle and we sat down on the edge of the pool. He began choosing among the mushrooms, flinging some in the water, and dropping others in the basket.

"There you are," said he, giving me the basket with the ones he had chosen. "Have them fried."

I wanted to ask him why the basket only contained halves of mushrooms, but I realized that the question would have been disrespectful and ran off, after thanking him warmly. I was just going to fry them for myself when I met the group of servants, and heard that all my halves were poisonous.

Sebastiana the nurse, when I told her the story, said, "The bad half of Medardo has returned. Now I wonder about this trial today."

That day there was to be a trial of a band of brigands arrested the day before by the castle constabulary. The brigands were from our estates and so it was for the Viscount to judge them. The trial was held and Medardo sat sideways on his chair chewing a fingernail. The brigands appeared in chains. The head of the band was the youth called Fiorfiero who had been the first to notice the Viscount's litter while pounding grapes. The injured parties appeared: they were a group of Tuscan knights who were passing through our woods on their way to Provence when they had been attacked and robbed by Fiorfiero and his band. Fiorfiero defended himself saying that those knights had come poaching on our land and he had stopped and disarmed them as poachers, since the constabulary had done nothing about them. It should be said that at the time assaults by brigands were very common, and laws were clement. Also, our parts were particularly suitable for brigandage, so that even some members of our family, especially in these turbulent times, would join brigand bands. As for smuggling, it was about the lightest crime imaginable.

But Sebastiana's apprehensions were well founded. Medardo condemned Fiorfiero and his whole band to die by hanging, as criminals guilty of armed rapine. But since those robbed were guilty of poaching he condemned them to die on the gibbet too. And to punish the constables who had appeared too late and not prevented either brigands or poachers from misbehaving, he decreed death by hanging for them too. There were about twenty altogether. This cruel sentence produced consternation in us all, not so much for the Tuscan gentry whom no one had seen until then, as for the brigands and constables who were generally well liked. Master Pietrochiodo, pack-saddle-maker and carpenter, was given the job of making the gibbet. He was a most conscientious worker who took great pains in all he did. With great sorrow, for two of the condemned were his relations, he built a gibbet ramificating like a tree, whose nooses all rose together, and were maneuvered by a single winch. It was such a big and ingenious machine that it could have hanged simultaneously even more people than those now condemned. The Viscount took advantage of this to hang ten cats alternating with every two criminals. The rigid corpses and cats' carcasses hung there for three days, and at first no one had the heart to look at them. But soon people noticed what a really imposing sight they were, and our own judgments and opinions began to vary, so that we were even sorry when it was decided to take them down and dismantle the big machine.

FOR me those were happy times, wandering through woods with Dr. Trelawney in search of fossil traces. Dr. Trelawney was English; he had reached our coasts after a shipwreck, astride a ship's barrel. All his life he had been a ship's doctor and made long and peril-ous journeys, some of them with the famous Captain Cook, though he had seen nothing of the world since he was always under hatches playing cards. On being shipwrecked among us he soon acquired a taste for a wine called *cancarone*, the harshest and heaviest in our parts, and now could not do without it, so that he always had a full water-flask of it slung over his shoulder. He had stayed on at Terralba and become our doctor; but he bothered little about the sick, only about his scientific researches, which kept him on the go—and me with him—through fields and woods by day and night. First came a crickets' disease caught by one cricket in a thousand and doing no particular harm. Dr. Trelawney wanted to examine them all and find the right cure. Next it was specimens of the time when our lands were covered by sea, and we would load up with pebbles and flints which, according to the doctor, had been fish in their time. Finally his last great passion: will-o'-the-wisps. He wanted to find a way of catching and keeping them, and with this aim in view we would spend nights wandering about our cemetery, waiting for one of those vague lights to go up among the mounds of earth and grass, when he would try to draw it towards us, make it follow us and then capture it, without its going out, in various receptacles with which we experimented: sacks, flasks, strawless demijohns, braziers, colanders. Dr. Trelawney had settled near the cemetery in a shack which had once been the grave-digger's in times of pomp and war and plague, when a man was needed on the job full time. There the doctor had set up his laboratory, with test tubes of every shape, to bottle the wisps, and nets like those for fishing to catch them; and retorts and crucibles in which he examined the why and wherefore of those pale little flames coming from the soil of cemeteries and the exhalations of corpses. But he was not a man to remain for long absorbed in studies. He would break off and come out, and then we would go hunting together for new phenomena of nature.

I was free as air since I had no parents and belonged to the category neither of servants nor masters. I was part of the Terralba family only by tardy recognition, but did not bear their name and no one had bothered to give me any education. My poor mother had been the Viscount Aiolfo's daughter, and Medardo's elder sister, but she had besmirched the family honor by eloping with a poacher who was my father. I was born in a poacher's hut in rough undergrowth by the woods, and shortly afterward my father was killed in some squabble, and pellagra put an end to my mother who had stayed in that wretched hut all alone. Then I was brought into the castle, as my grandfather Aiolfo took pity on me, and grew up under the care of the chief nurse, Sebastiana. I remember that when Medardo was still a boy and I was a small child he would sometimes let me take part in his games as if we were of equal rank. Then distance grew between us and I dropped to the level of a servant. Now in Dr. Trelawney I found a companion such as I had never had.

The doctor was sixty but about as tall as I. He had a face lined like an old chestnut, under tricorn and wig. His legs, with gaiters halfway up his thighs, looked long and disproportionate as a cricket's, the effect being emphasized by his long strides. He wore a dove-colored tunic with red facings, and slung across it, the bottle of *cancarone* wine.

His passion for will-o'-the-wisps made him take long night marches to the cemeteries of nearby villages, where at times flames were to be seen finer in color and size than those in our abandoned cemetery. But it was bad for us if our stalking was found out by locals. Once we were mistaken for sacrilegious thieves and were followed for miles by a group of men armed with forks and tridents.

Dr. Trelawney and I hopped from rock to rock, but heard the infuriated peasants getting closer behind. At a place called Grimace's Leap was a small bridge of tree trunks straddling a deep abyss. Instead of crossing over the doctor and I hid on a ledge of rock on the abyss's very edge, just in time as the peasants were right on our heels. They did not see us, and yelling, "Where are the swine?" rushed straight at the bridge. A crack, and they were flung screaming into the torrent far below. Trelawney's and my terror for our own skins changed to relief at danger escaped and then to terror again at the awful fate that had befallen our pursuers. We scarcely dared lean over and peer down into the darkness where the peasants had vanished. Then raising our eyes we looked at the remains of the little bridge; the trunks were still firmly in place, but they were broken in half as if sawn through. That could be the only explanation for thick wood giving way with such a clean break.

"There's the hand of *you know who* in this," said Dr. Trelawney, and I understood.

Just then we heard a quick clatter of hooves and on the verge of the precipice appeared a horse and a rider half wrapped in a black cloak. It was the Viscount Medardo, who was contemplating with his frozen triangular smile the tragic success of his trap, unforeseen perhaps by himself. He must certainly have wanted to kill us two off; instead of which, as it turned out, he had saved our lives. Trembling, we saw him gallop off on that thin horse, which went leaping away over the rocks as if born of a goat.

At that time my uncle always went round on horseback. He had gotten our saddle-maker Pietro-

chiodo to make him a special saddle with a stirrup
to which he could hitch himself, while the other
had a counterweight. A sword and crutch were slung
by the saddle. And so the Viscount galloped about,
wearing a plumed hat with a great brim which half
vanished under a wing of the ever-fluttering cloak.
Wherever the sound of his horse's hooves was heard,
everyone took to his heels—even more than when
Galateo the leper passed—and bore off children and
animals. They feared for their plants, as the Viscount's
wickedness spared no one and could burst at any
moment into the most unforeseen and incomprehensible actions.

He had never been ill, so never needed Dr. Trelawney's care. I don't know how the doctor would
have dealt with such an eventuality as he did his
very best to avoid ever hearing my uncle mentioned.
When he heard people talking about the Viscount
and his cruelty, Dr. Trelawney would shake his head
and curl a lip with a mutter of "Oh, oh, oh . . . zzt,
zzt, zzt!" It seemed that from the medical point of
view my uncle's case aroused no interest in him. But
I was beginning to think that he had become a doctor
only from family pressure or his own convenience,
and did not care a rap about the science of it. Perhaps
his career as ship's doctor had been due only to his
ability at card games, which made the most illustrious
navigators, particularly Captain Cook himself, con-
tend for him as partner.

One night Dr. Trelawney was fishing with a net
for will-o'-the-wisps in our ancient cemetery when
his eyes fell on Medardo of Terralba pasturing his

horse around the tombs. The doctor was much confused and alarmed, but the Viscount came nearer and
asked him in the defective pronunciation of his halved
mouth, "Are you looking for night butterflies, doctor?"

"Oh, m'lord," replied the doctor in a faint voice.
"Oh, not exactly butterflies, m'lord . . . Will-o'-the-
wisps, you know, will-o'-the-wisps . . ."

"Ah, will-o'-the-wisps, eh? I've often wondered
about their origin too."

"They have been the subject of my modest studies
for some time, m'lord . . ." said Trelawney, encouraged
by his benevolent tone.

Medardo twisted his angular half face into a
smile, the skin taut as a skull's. "You deserve all assistance in your studies," he said to him. "A pity that this
cemetery is so abandoned, and thus no good for
will-o'-the-wisps. But I promise you that I'll see
about helping you as much as I can tomorrow."

Next day was the one allocated for administering
justice, and the Viscount condemned a dozen peasants
to death, because according to his computation they
had not handed over the whole proportion of crops
due from them to the castle. The dead men were
buried in a common grave, and the cemetery blossomed
every night with numerous will-o'-the-wisps. Dr.
Trelawney was terrified by this help, useful as it was
to his studies.

With all these tragic developments Master Pietrochiodo was producing greatly improved gibbets. Now

they were real masterpieces of carpentry and mechanics, as were also the racks, winches and other instruments of torture by which the Viscount Medardo tore confessions from the accused. I was often in Pietrochiodo's workshop, as it was a fine sight to watch him at work with such ability and enthusiasm. But a sorrow always weighed on the saddler's heart. The scaffolds he was constructing were for innocent men. "How can I manage to get orders for work as delicate, but with a different purpose? What new mechanisms would I enjoy making more?" But finding these questions coming to no conclusions, he tried to thrust them out of his mind and settle down to making his instruments as fine and ingenious as possible.

"Just forget the purpose for which they're used," he said to me, "and look at them as pieces of mechanism. You see how fine they are?"

I looked at that architecture of beams, crisscross of ropes, links of capstans and pulleys, and tried not to see tortured bodies on them, but the more I tried the more I found myself thinking of them, and said to Pietrochiodo: "How can I forget?"

"How indeed, my lad?" replied he. "How d'you think I can, then?"

But with all their agonies and terrors, those days had times of delight. The loveliest hour was when the sun was high and the sea golden and the chickens sang as they laid their eggs and from the lane came the sound of the leper's horn. The leper would pass every morning to collect alms for his companions in misfortune. He was called Galateo, and round his neck he wore a hunting horn whose sound warned us from a distance of his arrival. Women would hear the horn and lay out eggs or melons or tomatoes and sometimes a little rabbit on the edge of the wall; and then they would run off and hide, taking their children, for no one should be out in the open when a leper goes by: leprosy can be caught from a distance and it's dangerous even to look at one. Preceded by notes on his horn, Galateo would come slowly along the deserted lanes, with a tall stick in his hand and a long tattered robe touching the ground. He had long yellow hair and a round white face already eaten away by leprosy. He gathered up the gifts, put them in his knapsack and called his thanks towards the houses of the hidden peasants in honeyed tones that always included some jolly double meaning.

In those days leprosy was very prevalent in districts near the sea, and near us was a village called Pratofungo, inhabited only by lepers, for whom we were bound to produce gifts which Galateo gathered up. When anyone from the sea or country caught leprosy, he left relatives and friends and went to Pratofungo to spend the rest of his life waiting for the disease to devour him. There were rumors of great merrymaking to greet each new arrival. From afar song and music was heard coming from the lepers' houses till nightfall.

Many things were said of Pratofungo although no healthy person had ever been there, but rumors were agreed in saying that life there was a perpetual party. Before becoming a leper colony the village had been a great place for prostitutes and visited by sailors of every race and religion; and the women there, it seemed, still kept the licentious habits of those times. The lepers did no work on the land, except for a vineyard of strawberry grapes whose juice kept them the whole year round in a state of simmering tipsiness. The lepers spent most of their time playing strange instruments of their own invention, such as harps with little bells attached to the strings, and singing in falsetto, and painting eggs with daubs of every color as if for a perpetual Easter. And so, whiling away the time with sweet music, their disfigured faces hung round with garlands of jasmine, they forgot the human community from which their disease had cut them off.

No local doctor had ever taken on the care of the lepers, but when Trelawney settled amongst us, some hoped that he might feel like dedicating his lore to healing that running sore in our locality. I shared the same hopes too, in my childish way; for some time I had been longing to get into Pratofungo and attend those lepers' parties, and had the doctor done any experimenting with his drugs on those wretches he might have allowed me to accompany him into the village sometimes. But none of this ever happened. As soon as he heard Galateo's horn Dr. Trelawney ran off at full speed and no one seemed more afraid of contagion than he. Sometimes I tried to question him on the nature of the disease, but he would make evasive or muted replies, as if the very word "leper" put him out.

Actually I can't think why we were so determined to think of him as a doctor. He was very attentive to animals, particularly small ones, or to stones or natural phenomena, but human beings and their infirmities filled him with dismay and disgust. He had a horror of blood, he would only touch the sick with the tips of his fingers, and when faced with serious cases plunged his nose in a silk bandanna dipped in vinegar. He was shy as a girl, and blushed at the sight of a naked body; if it was a woman's he would stutter and keep his eyes lowered. In all his long journeys over the oceans he never seemed to have known women. Luckily for us, in those times births were matters for midwives and not doctors, otherwise I wonder how he would have managed.

Into my uncle's head now came the notion of arson. At night all of a sudden a haystack of wretched peasants, or a tree cut for fuel, or a whole wood would burn. Then we would spend the whole night passing buckets of water from hand to hand in order to put out the flames. The victims were always poor unfortunates who had fallen out with the Viscount, either because of one of his increasingly severe and unjust orders or because of the dues he had doubled.

From burning other things he then began setting
fire to houses. It was thought that he came up close
at night, threw burning brands on roofs and then
rushed off on horseback, but no one ever managed
to catch him in the act. Once two old people died.
Once a boy had his brains fried. The peasants grew
to hate him more and more. His most stubborn
enemies were some families of Huguenots who were
living in huts up on Col Gerbido. Their men kept
guard all night to prevent fires.

One night without any plausible reason he even
went under the houses of Pratofungo, whose roofs
were thatched, and threw burning brands at them. A
characteristic of lepers is to feel no pain when scorched,
and had they been caught by the flames in their
sleep they would never have woken again. But as
the Viscount galloped away he heard a tune on a
violin from the village behind him; the inhabitants
of Pratofungo were still up and intent on their fun.
They all got a little scorched, but felt no ill effects
and amused themselves in their own way. The fire
was soon put out; and their homes, perhaps because
so impregnated with leprosy, suffered little damage
from the flames.

Medardo's evil nature even turned him against
his own personal property, the castle itself. A fire went
up in the servants' wing, and spread amid the loud
shrieks of those trapped there, while the Viscount
was seen galloping off into the country. It was an
attempt on the life of his nurse and foster mother
Sebastiana. With the stubborn bossiness that women

claim over those they have seen as children, Sebastiana was constantly reproving the Viscount for his every misdeed, even when all were convinced that his nature forced him to acts of insane and irreparable cruelty. Sebastiana was pulled out from the burning walls in a very bad state and had to stay in bed for days to heal her burns.

One night the door of the room in which she was lying opened and the Viscount appeared by her bed.

"What are those marks on your face, nurse?" said Medardo, pointing at her burns.

"Marks of your sins, son," said the old woman calmly.

"Your skin is all speckled and scored. What ails you, nurse?"

"My ails are nothing, son, compared to those awaiting you in hell unless you mend your ways."

"You must get well soon; I would not like to hear of you going round with this disease on you."

"I'm not out for a husband, that I need bother about my looks. A good conscience is enough for me. I only wish you could say the same."

"And yet your bridegroom is waiting to bear you off with him, you know!"

"Do not deride old age, my son, you who have had your youth ruined."

"I do not jest. Hark, nurse; there is your bridegroom playing beneath your window . . ."

Sebastiana listened and from outside the castle heard the sound of the leper's horn.

Next day Medardo sent for Dr. Trelawney.

"Suspicious marks have appeared on the face of our old servant, I don't know how," he said to the doctor. "We're all afraid it's leprosy. Doctor, we entrust ourselves to the light of your knowledge."

Trelawney bowed and stuttered.

"M'duty, m'lord . . . at your orders, as always, m'lord . . ."

He turned, slipped out of the castle, got himself a small barrel of *cancarone* and vanished into the woods. He was not seen again for a week. When he got back Sebastiana had been sent to the leper village.

One evening at dusk she left the castle, veiled and dressed in black, with a bundle on her arm. She knew that her fate was sealed; she must take the road to Pratofungo. Leaving the room where she had been kept till then, she found the passages and stairs deserted. Down she went, across the courtyard, out into the country; all was deserted, everyone at her passage withdrew and hid. She heard a hunting horn sounding a low call on two notes only. On the path ahead of her was Galateo with the mouthpiece of his instrument raised to the sky. With slow steps the nurse advanced. The path went towards the setting sun. Galateo moved far ahead of her. Every now and then he stopped as if gazing at the bumble bees amid the leaves, raised his horn and played a sad note. The nurse looked at the flowers and banks that she was leaving, sensed behind hedges the presence of people avoiding her, and walked on. Alone, Galateo a long way behind, she reached Pratofungo, and as the village gates closed behind her harps and violins began to play.

Dr. Trelawney had disappointed me a lot. Not having moved a finger to prevent old Sebastiana from being condemned to the leper colony—though knowing that her marks were not those of leprosy—was a sign of cowardice, and for the first time I felt a sense of aversion for the doctor. On top of this he had not taken me with him when he ran off into the woods, though knowing how useful I would have been as a hunter of squirrels and finder of raspberries. Now I no longer enjoyed going with him for will-o'-the-wisps as before, and often went around alone, on the lookout for new companions.

The people who most attracted me now were the Huguenots up on Col Gerbido. They were people who had escaped from France, where the King had those who followed their religion cut into small pieces. While crossing the mountains they had lost their books and sacred objects, and now had neither Bibles to read from nor Mass to say nor hymns to sing nor prayers to recite. Suspicious, like all those who have passed through persecutions and live amid people of a different faith, they had refused to accept any religious book, or listen to any advice on how to conduct their rites. If someone came looking for them saying he was a fellow Huguenot, they suspected that

he might be a Papal agent in disguise, and shut themselves off in silence. So they cultivated the harsh
lands of Col Gerbido; they overworked men and
women, from before dawn till after dusk, in the hope
of being illuminated by Grace. Inexpert in what con-
stituted sin, they multiplied their prohibitions lest
they make mistakes, and were reduced to giving each
other constant severe glances in case the least gesture
betrayed a blameworthy intention. With confused
memories of theological disputations, they avoided
naming God or using any other religious expression,
for fear of sacrilege. So they followed no rites and
probably did not even dare formulate thoughts on
matters of faith, though preserving an air of grave ab-
sorption as if these were constantly in their minds.
But with time the rules of their agricultural labors had
acquired a value equal to those of the Command-
ments, as had the habits of thrift and diligent house-
keeping to which they were forced.

They were all one great family, with lots of grandchildren and in-laws, all tall and knobbly, and they
worked the land always formally dressed in buttoned
black, the men in wide-brimmed hats and the women
in white kerchiefs. The men wore long beards and
always went round with slung blunderbusses, but it
was said that none of them had ever fired a shot, except at sparrows, as it was forbidden by the Com-
mandments.

From chalky terraces with a few stunted vines
and wretched crops would rise the voice of old
Ezekiel, forever shouting with fists raised to the sky,

his white goatee beard trembling, eyes rolling under his tubular hat. "Famine and plague! Famine and plague!" he would yell at his family bent over their work, "Hoe harder, Jonah! Tear at those weeds, Susanna! Spread that manure, Tobias!" and give out thousands of orders and rebukes in the bitter tone of one addressing a bunch of inept wasters. Every time, after shouting out the innumerable things they must do to prevent the land going to ruin, he would begin doing them himself, pushing away the others around, still shouting, "Famine and plague!"

His wife on the other hand never shouted, and seemed, unlike the others, secure in a secret religion of her own, which was fixed to the smallest details but never mentioned by so much as a single word to anyone. She would just stare, her eyes all pupils, and only say, through set lips, "D'you think that's right, Sister Rachel? D'you think that's right, Brother Aaron?" for the rare smiles to vanish from her family's mouths and their grave intent expressions to return.

One evening I arrived at Col Gerbido while the Huguenots were praying. Not that they pronounced any words or joined hands or knelt; they were standing in a row in the vineyard, men on one side and women on the other, with old Ezekiel at the end, his beard on his chest. They looked straight in front of them, with clenched hands hanging from long knobbly arms, but though they seemed absorbed they had not lost awareness of what was going on around them; and Tobias put out a hand and tweaked a caterpillar off a vine, Rachel crushed a snail with her nailed boot, and Ezekiel himself suddenly took off his hat to frighten sparrows on the crops.

Then they intoned a psalm. They did not remember the words, only the tune, and even that not well, and often someone went off key or maybe they all were off the whole time, but they never stopped, and on finishing one verse started another, always without pronouncing any words.

I felt a tug at my arm; it was little Esau signing me to be quiet and come with him. Esau was my age; he was old Ezekiel's last son. The only look he had of his parents was their hard, tense expression, with a sly malice of his own. We went off on all fours through the vineyard, with him saying, "They'll be at it another half hour, you see. Come and look at my lair."

Esau's lair was secret. He used to hide there so that his family could not find him and send him to look after goats or take snails off the crops. He would spend entire days there doing nothing, while his father went searching and calling for him throughout the countryside.

Esau gave me a pipe and told me to smoke it. He lit one for himself and drew great mouthfuls with an enthusiasm I had never seen in a boy. It was the first time I had smoked; it soon made me feel sick and I stopped. To pull me together Esau drew out a bottle of *grappa* and poured me a glassful, which made me cough and wrung my guts. He drank it as if it were water.

"It takes a lot to get drunk," he said.

"Where did you find all these things you have here in your lair?" I asked him.

Esau made a gesture of clawing the air, "Stolen!"

He had put himself at the head of a band of Catholic boys who were sacking the country. They not only stripped the trees of fruit, but went into houses and hen coops. And they swore stronger and more often even than Master Pietrochiodo. They knew every swear word, Catholic and Huguenot, and exchanged them freely.

"There's a lot of other sins I commit too," he explained to me. "I bear false witness, I forget to water the beans, I don't respect father and mother, I come home late. Now I want to commit every sin there is, even the ones people say I'm not old enough to understand."

"Every sin?" I asked him. "Killing too?"

He shrugged his shoulders. "Killing's not in my line now, it's no use."

"My uncle kills and has people killed just for fun, they say," I exclaimed, just for something with which to counterbalance Esau.

Esau spat. "A thug's game," he said.

Then it thundered and outside the lair it began to rain.

"They'll be on the lookout for you at home," I said to Esau. Nobody was ever on the lookout for me, but I had seen other boys being sought by parents, particularly in bad weather, and I thought that was something important.

"Let's wait for it to stop," said Esau, "and have a game of dice."

He pulled out the dice and a heap of money. I had no money, so I gambled my whistles, knives and catapults, and lost the lot.

"Don't let it get you down," said Esau eventually. "I cheat, you know."

Outside—thunder, lightning and torrential rain. Esau's cave was flooding. He salvaged his cigars and other things and said, "It'll pour all night, better run and shelter at home."

We were soaked and muddy when we reached old Ezekiel's hut. The Huguenots were sitting around the table, illuminated by a flickering candle, and were trying to remember episodes from the Bible, taking great care to narrate them as if they had once read them.

"Famine and plague!" Ezekiel shouted, and banged a fist on the table so hard it put out the light just when his son Esau appeared in the doorway with me.

My teeth began chattering. Esau shrugged his shoulders. Outside all the thunder and lightning seemed to be unloading on Col Gerbido. As they were rekindling the light the old man with raised fists enumerated his son's sins as the foulest ever committed by any human being, but he only knew a small part of them. The mother nodded mutely, and all the other sons and sons-in-law and daughters-in-law and grandchildren listened, chins on chest and faces hidden in their hands. Esau was chewing away at an apple as if the sermon did not concern him. What with the thunder and Ezekiel's voice I was trembling like a reed.

The diatribe was interrupted by the return of the men on guard, using sacks for hoods, who were all soaking wet. The Huguenots kept guard all night long in turns, armed with muskets, scythes and pitch-forks, to prevent the prowling incursions of the Viscount, now their declared enemy.

"Father! Ezekiel!" said these Huguenots. " 'Tis a night for wolves. For sure the Lame One won't come. May we return home, Father?"

"Are there no signs of the Maimed One?" asked Ezekiel.

"No, Father, except for the smell of burning left by the lightning. 'Tis not a night for the Bereft One."

"Stay here and change your clothes then. May the storm bring peace to the Sideless One and to us."

The Lame One, the Maimed One, the Bereft One and the Sideless One were some of the appellations given by the Huguenots to my uncle. Never once did I hear them call him by his real name. These remarks showed a kind of intimacy with the Viscount, as if they knew a great deal about him, almost as if he were an old enemy. They would exchange brief phrases accompanied by winks and laughs. "Ha ha! The Maimed One . . . Just like him, ha ha! The Half-Deaf One . . ." as if to them all of Medardo's dark follies were clear and foreseeable.

They were talking thus when a fist was heard

knocking at the door in the storm. "Who knocks in this weather?" said Ezekiel. "Quick, open."

They opened the door and there on the threshold was the Viscount, standing on his one leg, wrapped in a dripping cloak, his plumed hat soaked with rain.

"I have tied up my horse in your stall," he said. "Will you give me hospitality too? It's a bad night for a traveller."

Everyone looked at Ezekiel. I had hidden myself beneath the table lest my uncle should discover that I frequented this enemy house.

"Sit down by the fire," said Ezekiel. "In this house a guest is always welcome."

Near the threshold was a heap of sheets, the kind used for stretching under trees to gather olives; there Medardo lay down and went to sleep.

In the dark the Huguenots gathered around Ezekiel. "Father, we have the Lame One in our hands now!" they whispered to each other. "Must we let him go? Must we let him commit other crimes against innocent folk? Ezekiel, has the hour not come for the Buttockless One to pay the price?"

The old man raised his fists to the ceiling. "Famine and plague!" he shouted, if someone can be said to shout who scarcely emits a sound but does it with all his strength. "No guest has ever been ill-treated in our house. I myself will mount guard to protect his sleep."

And with his musket ready he took his place by the sleeping Viscount. Medardo's eye opened. "What are you doing there, Master Ezekiel?"

"I protect your sleep, guest. You are hated by many."

"That I know," said the Viscount. "I do not sleep at the castle as I fear the servants might kill me as I lie."

"Nor do they love you in my house, Master Medardo. But tonight you will be respected."

The Viscount was silent for some time, and then said, "Ezekiel, I wish to be converted to your religion."

The old man said nothing.

"I am surrounded by men I do not trust," went on Medardo, "I should like to rid myself of the lot and call the Huguenots to the castle. You, Master Ezekiel, will be my minister. I will declare Terralba to be Huguenot territory and we will start a war against the Catholic princes. You and your family shall be the leaders. Are you agreed, Ezekiel? Can you convert me?"

The old man stood there straight and motion-less, his big chest crossed by the bandolier of his gun. "Too many things have we forgotten in our religion," said he, "for me to dare convert anyone. I will remain in my own territory, according to my own conscience, you in yours with yours."

The Viscount raised himself on his elbow. "You know, Ezekiel, that I have not yet reported to the Inquisition the presence of heretics in my domain, and that your heads sent as a present to our Bishop would at once bring me back to favor with the Curia?"

"Our heads are still on our necks, sir," said the

old man. "But there is something else far more difficult to tear from us."

Medardo leapt to his foot and opened the door. "Rather would I sleep under that oak tree there than in the house of enemies." And off he hopped into the rain.

The old man called the others. "Sons, it was written that the Lame One was to come and visit us. Now he's gone; the way to our house is clear. Do not despair, sons; one day perhaps a better traveller will pass."

All the bearded Huguenots and the coiffed women bowed their heads.

"And even if no one comes," added Ezekiel's wife, "we will stay at our posts."

At that moment a streak of lightning rent the sky, and thunder made the tiles and the stones of the wall quiver. Tobias shouted "The lightning has struck the oak tree. It is burning!"

They ran out with their lanterns and saw the great tree carbonized down through the middle, from top to roots, and the other half intact. Far off under the rain they heard a horse's hooves and by a lightning flash caught a glimpse of the cloaked figure of its thin rider.

"Father, you have saved us," said the Huguenots. "Thank you, Ezekiel."

The sky cleared to the east and it was dawn.

Esau called me aside. "You see what fools they are!" he whispered. "Look what I've done meanwhile," and he showed me a handful of glittering objects. "I took all the gold studs on the saddle while the horse was tied in the stall. You see what fools they are, not to have thought of it."

I did not like Esau's ways, and those of his relations I found oppressive. So I preferred being on my own and going to the shore to gather limpets and catch crabs. While I was on top of a little rock trying to corner a small crab, in the calm water below me I saw the reflection of a blade above my head, and fell into the sea from fright.

"Catch hold of this," said my uncle, for it was he who had come up behind me. And he tried to make me grasp his sword by the blade.

"No, I'll do it by myself," I replied, and clambered up onto a crag separated by a limb of water from the rest of the rocks.

"Are you out for crabs?" said Medardo, "I'm out for baby octopus," and he showed me his catch. They were fat baby octopuses, brown and white. Although they had been cut in two with a sword, they were still moving their tentacles.

"If only I could halve every whole thing like this," said my uncle, lying face down on the rocks, stroking the convulsive half of an octopus, "so that everyone could escape from his obtuse and ignorant wholeness. I was whole and all things were natural and confused to me, stupid as the air; I thought I was seeing all and it was only the outside rind. If you

ever become a half of yourself, and I hope you do for
your own sake, my boy, you'll understand things
beyond the common intelligence of brains that are
whole. You'll have lost half of yourself and of the
world, but the remaining half will be a thousand times
deeper and more precious. And you too would find
yourself wanting everything to be halved like yourself,
because beauty and knowledge and justice only exists
in what has been cut to shreds."

"Uh, uh!" I kept on saying, "What a lot of crabs
there are here!" and I pretended to be interested only
in my catch, so as to keep as far as possible from
my uncle's sword. I did not return to land until he
had moved off with his octopuses. But the echo of
his words went on disturbing me and I could find
no escape from this frenzy of his for halving.
Wherever I turned, Trelawney, Pietrochiodo, the
Huguenots, the lepers, we were all under the sign of
the halved man, he was the master whom we served
and from whom we could not succeed in freeing
ourselves.

{ 6 }

HITCHED to the saddle of his high-jumping horse, Medardo of Terralba would be out early, up and down bluffs, leaning over precipices to gaze over a valley with the eye of a bird of prey. That is how he came to see Pamela in the middle of a field with her goats.

The Viscount said to himself, "With all my acute emotions I have nothing that corresponds to what whole people call love. If an emotion so silly is yet so important to them, then whatever may correspond in me will surely be very grand and awesome." So he decided to fall in love with Pamela, as she lay, plump and barefoot, in a simple pink dress, face downwards in the grass, dozing, chatting to the goats and sniffing flowers.

But thoughts thus coldly formulated should not deceive us. At the sight of Pamela, Medardo had sensed a vague stirring of the blood, something he had not felt for ages, and he rushed into these rationalizations with a kind of alarmed haste.

On her way home at midday Pamela noticed

that all the daisies in the fields had only half their petals and the other half had been stripped off. "Dear me!" she said to herself. "Of all the girls in the valley, that this should happen to me!" For she realized that the Viscount had fallen in love with her. She picked all the halved daisies, took them home and put them among the pages of her Mass book.

That afternoon she went to the Nun's Field to pasture her ducks and let them swim in the pond. The field was covered with white parsnip blossoms, but these flowers had also suffered the fate of the daisies, as if part of each had been cut away with a snip of scissors. "Dear, oh dear me!" she said to herself. "So it's really me he wants!" And she gathered the halved parsnip blossoms in a bunch, to slip them into the frame of the mirror over her chest of drawers.

Then she put it out of her mind, tied her plaits round her head, took off her dress and had a bathe in the pond with her ducks.

That evening as she went home the fields were full of dandelion flowers. And Pamela saw that they had lost their fluff on only one side, as if someone had lain on the ground and blown just on one side, or with only half a mouth. Pamela gathered some of those halved white spheres, breathed on them and their soft fluff floated away. "Dear, oh dearie dear!" said she to herself. "He wants me, he really does. How will it all end?"

Pamela's cottage was so small that once the goats had been let onto the first floor and the ducks onto the ground floor there was no more room. It was surrounded by bees, for the family also kept hives. The subsoil was so full of ants that a hand put down anywhere came up all black and swarming with them. Because of this Pamela's mother slept in the haystack, her father in an empty barrel and Pamela in a hammock slung between a fig and an olive tree.

On the threshold Pamela stopped. There was a dead butterfly. A wing and half the body had been crushed by a stone. Pamela let out a shriek and called her father and mother.

"Who's been here?" said Pamela.

"Our Viscount passed by a short time ago," said her father and mother. "He said he was chasing a butterfly that had stung him."

"When has a butterfly ever stung anyone?" said Pamela.

"We've been wondering too."

"The truth is," said Pamela, "that the Viscount has fallen in love with me and we must be ready for the worst."

"Uh, uh, don't get a swollen head now, don't exaggerate," answered the old couple, as old folk are apt to answer when the young don't do the same to them.

Next morning when Pamela got to the stone on which she usually sat when pasturing her goats, she let out a cry. It was all smeared with ghastly remains; half a bat and half a jellyfish, one oozing black blood and the other shiny matter, one with the wing spread and the other with soft gelatinous edges. The goatgirl realized that this was a message. It meant: rendezvous

on the seashore tonight. Pamela took her courage in
both hands and went.

By the sea she sat on pebbles and listened to the
rustle of white-flecked waves. Then came a clatter
on the pebbles and Medardo galloped along the shore.
He stopped, unhitched, got off his saddle.

"Pamela, I have decided to fall in love with you,"
he said to her.

"And is that why," she exclaimed, "you're torturing all these creatures of nature?"

"Pamela," sighed the Viscount, "we have no
other language in which to express ourselves but that.
Every meeting between two creatures in this world
is a mutual rending. Come with me, for I have knowledge of such pain, and you'll be safer with me than
with anyone else; for I do harm as do all, but the
difference between me and others is that I have a
steady hand."

And will you tear me in two as you have the
daisies and the jellyfish?"

"I don't know what I'll do with you. Certainly
my having you will make possible certain things I
never imagined. I'll take you to the castle and keep
you there and no one else will ever see you and we'll
have days and months to realize what we should do
and we'll invent new ways of being together."

Pamela was lying on the sand and Medardo had
knelt beside her. As he spoke he waved his hand all
around her, but without touching her.

"Well, first I must know what you'll do to me.

You can give me a sample now and then I'll decide whether to come to the castle or not."

The Viscount slowly drew his thin bony hand near Pamela's cheek. The hand was trembling and it was not clear if it was stretched to caress or to scratch. But it had not yet touched her when he suddenly drew it back and got up.

"It's at the castle I want you," he said, hitching himself back on to his horse. "I'm going to prepare the tower you will live in. I will leave you another day to think it over, then you must make up your mind."

So saying he spurred off along the beach.

Next day Pamela climbed up the mulberry tree as usual to gather fruit, and heard a moaning and fluttering among the branches. She nearly fell off from fright. A cock was tied on a branch by its wings and was being devoured by great hairy blue caterpillars; a nest of evil insects that live on pines had settled right on the top.

This was another of the Viscount's ghastly messages, of course. Pamela's interpretation was: "Tomorrow at dawn in the wood."

With the excuse of gathering a sackful of pine cones Pamela went up into the woods, and Medardo appeared from behind a tree trunk leaning on his crutch.

"Well," he asked Pamela, "have you made up your mind to come to the castle?"

Pamela was lying stretched out on pine needles. "I've made up my mind not to go," she said, scarcely turning. "If you want me, come and meet me here in the woods."

"You'll come to the castle. The tower where you're to live is ready and you'll be its only mistress."

"You want to keep me prisoner there and then get me burnt in a fire or maybe eaten up by rats. No, no. I told you, I'll be yours if you like but here on the pine needles."

The Viscount had crouched down near her head. In his hand he had a pine needle, which he brought close on her neck and passed all round it. Pamela felt goose flesh come over her, but lay still. She saw the Viscount's face bent over her, that profile which remained a profile even when seen from the front, and that half set of teeth bared in a scissors-like smile. Medardo clutched the pine needle in his fist and broke it. He got up. "I want you shut in the castle, yes, shut in the castle!"

Pamela realized she could risk it, so she waved her bare feet in the air and said, "Here in the wood I wouldn't say no; I wouldn't do it all shut up—not if I were dead."

"I'll get you there!" said Medardo, putting his hand on the shoulder of his horse which had come up as if it were passing there by chance. He leapt on the saddle and spurred off down a forest track.

That night Pamela slept in her hammock swung between olive and fig, and in the morning, horrors! she found a little bleeding carcass in her lap. It was a half a squirrel, cut as usual longways, but with its fluffy tail intact.

"Poor me!" said she to her parents. "This Viscount just won't leave me alone."

Her father and mother passed the carcass of the squirrel from hand to hand.

"But," said her father, "he's left the tail whole. That may be a good sign."

"Maybe he's beginning to be good . . ." said her mother.

"He always cuts everything in two," said her father, "but the loveliest thing on a squirrel, its tail, he respects that . . ."

"Maybe that's what the message means," exclaimed her mother. "He'll respect what's good and beautiful about you."

Pamela put her hands in her hair. "What things to hear from my own father and mother! There's something behind this; the Viscount has spoken to you . . ."

"Not spoken," said her father. "But he's let us know that he wants to visit us and will take an interest in our wretched state."

"Father, if he comes to talk to you, open up the hives and set the bees on him."

"Daughter, maybe Master Medardo is getting better . . ." said the old woman.

"Mother, if he comes to talk to you, tie him to the ant heap and leave him there."

That night the haystack where the mother slept caught fire and the barrel where the father slept came apart. In the morning the two old folk were staring at the remains when the Viscount appeared.

"I must apologize for alarming you last night," said he, "but I didn't quite know how to approach the subject. The fact is that I am attracted to your daughter Pamela and want to take her to the castle. So I wish to ask you formally to hand her over to me. Her life will change, and so will yours."

"You can imagine how pleased we'd be, my lord!" said the old man. "But if you knew what a character my daughter has! Why she told us to set the bees from the hives on you . . ."

"Think of it, my lord . . ." said the mother, "why she told us to tie you to our ant heap . . ."

Luckily Pamela came home early that day. She found her father and mother tied up and gagged, one on the beehive, the other on the ant heap. And it was lucky that the bees knew the old man and the ants had other things to do than bite the old woman. So Pamela was able to save them both.

"You see just how good the Viscount's got, eh?" said Pamela.

But the two old people were plotting something. Next day they tied up Pamela and locked her in with the animals, then they went off to the castle to tell the Viscount that if he wanted their daughter he could send down for her as they for their part were ready to hand her over.

But Pamela knew how to talk to her creatures. The ducks pecked her free from the ropes, and the goats butted down the door. Off Pamela ran, taking her favorite goat and duck. She set up house in the wood, living in a cave known only to her and to a child who brought her food and news.

That child was myself. Life was fine with Pamela in the woods. I brought her fruit, cheese and fried fish and in exchange she gave me cups of goat's milk and duck's eggs. When she bathed in pools and streams I stood guard so no one should see her.

Sometimes my uncle passed through the woods, but he kept at a distance, though showing his presence in his usual grim way. Sometimes a shower of stones would graze Pamela and her goat and duck; sometimes the trunk of a pine tree on which she was leaning gave way, undermined at its base by blows of a hatchet; sometimes a spring would be fouled by the remains of slaughtered animals.

My uncle had now taken to hunting with a cross-bow, which he succeeded in maneuvering with his one arm. But he had got even grimmer and thinner, as if new agonies were gnawing at that remnant of a body of his.

One day Dr. Trelawney was going through the fields with me when the Viscount came towards us on horseback and nearly ran him down. The horse stopped with a hoof on the Englishman's chest. My uncle said, "Can you explain, doctor; I have a feeling as if the leg I've not got were tired from a long walk. What can that mean?"

Trelawney was confused and stuttered as usual, and the Viscount spurred off. But the question must have struck the doctor, who began thinking it over, holding his head in his hands. Never had I seen him take such an interest in a case of human ills.

{ 7 }

AROUND Pratofungo grew bushes of mint and hedges of rosemary, and it was not clear if these were wild or the paths of some herb garden. I used to wander round them breathing in the laden air and trying to find some way of reaching old Sebastiana.

Since Sebastiana had vanished along the track leading to the leper village, I remembered that I was an orphan more often. I despaired of ever getting news of her; I asked Galateo, calling out to him from the top of a tree I had climbed when he passed, but Galateo was no friend of children, who sometimes used to throw live lizards at him from treetops, and he only gave me jeering and incomprehensible replies in that treacly squeaky voice of his. Now to my curiosity to enter Pratofungo was added a yearning to see the old nurse again, and I was forever meandering around the ordoriferous bushes.

Once from a tangle of thyme rose a figure in a light-colored robe and straw hat, which walked off towards the village. It was an old leper, and wanting to ask him about the nurse I got close enough for him to hear me without shouting and said, "Hey, there, sir leper!"

But at that moment, perhaps woken by my words, right by me rose another figure, who sat up and stretched. His face was all scaly like dried bark, and he had a sparse woolly white beard. He took a whistle out of his pocket and blew a jeering blast in my direction. I realized then that the sunny afternoon was full of lepers lying hidden in the bushes; now very slowly they began rising to their feet in their light-colored robes and they walked against the sun towards Pratofungo, holding musical instruments or gardening tools with which they set up a great din. I had drawn away from the bearded man, but nearly bumped right into a noseless leper combing his hair among the laurels, and however much I went jumping off through the undergrowth I kept on running into other lepers and began to realize that the only direction I could move was towards Pratofungo, whose thatched roofs stuck over with eagles' feathers were now quite close, at the foot of the slope.

Only now and again did the lepers pay me any attention, with winks of the eye and notes of the mouth organ, but I felt that the real center of that march was myself, and that they were accompanying me to Pratofungo as if I were a captured animal. The house walls in the village were painted mauve and at a window a half-dressed woman with mauve marks on face and breasts was calling out, "The gardeners are back!" and was playing on a lyre. Other women now appeared at windows and balconies waving tambourines and singing, "Gardeners, welcome back!"

I was being very careful to keep in the middle of the lane and not touch anyone, but I found myself at a kind of crossroads, with lepers all round me, men and women, sitting out on the thresholds of their houses, dressed in faded rags and showing tumors and intimate parts, their hair stuck with hawthorn and anemone blossoms.

The lepers were holding a little concert, to all appearances in my honor. Some were bending their violins towards me with exaggerated scrapes of the bow, others made frogs' faces as soon as I looked at them, others held out strange puppets that moved up and down on strings. The concert was made up of these varying and discordant gestures and sounds, but there was a kind of jingle they kept on repeating. "Stainless was he, till he went out to blackberry."

"I'm looking for my nurse old Sebastiana," I shouted. "Can you tell me where she is?"

They burst out laughing in a knowing malicious way.

"Sebastiana!" I called, "Sebastiana! Where are you?"

"There, child," said a leper, "now be good, child," and he pointed to a door.

The door opened and out came a woman with an olive skin, maybe a Moor, half naked and tattooed with eagles' wings, who began a licentious dance. I did not quite understand what happened next; men and women flung themselves on each other and began what I afterwards realized was an orgy.

I was making myself as small as possible when

suddenly through the groups appeared old Sebastiana.

"Foul swine!" she cried. "Have some regard for an innocent soul, at least."

She took me by a hand and drew me away while they went on chanting, "Stainless was he, till he went out to blackberry!"

Sebastiana was wearing a light-colored mauve robe like a nun's and already had a few marks blotching her unlined cheeks. I was happy at finding the nurse, but in despair as she had taken me by the hand and must have given me leprosy. I told her so.

"Don't worry," replied Sebastiana. "My father was a pirate and my grandfather a hermit. I know the virtues of every herb against the Moors' diseases. They sting themselves here with marjoram and mallow, but I quietly make my own decoctions from borage and water cress which prevent my getting leprosy as long as I live."

"What about those marks on your face, nurse?" asked I, much relieved but still not quite convinced.

"Greek resin. To make them think I have leprosy too. Come here now and I'll give you a drink of my piping hot tisane, for one can't take too many precautions when going about places like these."

She had taken me off to her home, a shack a little apart, clean, with washing hung out to dry; and there we talked.

"How's Medardo? How's Medardo?" she kept on asking me, and every time I spoke she interrupted with, "Ah the rascal! Ah the scoundrel! In love! Ah poor girl! And here, you can't imagine what it's like here! What they waste! To think of all the things we deprive ourselves to give Galateo, and what they do with them! That Galateo is a good-for-nothing, anyway! A bad lot, and not the only one! What they are up to at night! And by day, too! Those women! Never have I seen such shameless creatures! If they'd only mend their clothes! Filthy and ragged! Oh, I told them so to their faces . . . And d'you know their answer?"

Delighted with this visit to the nurse, off I went the next day to fish for eels. I set my line in a pool of the stream and fell asleep as I waited. I don't know how long my sleep lasted; a sound awoke me. I opened my eyes, saw a hand raised over my head, and in the hand a red hairy spider. I turned and there was my uncle in his black cloak.

I gave a start of terror, but at that moment the spider bit my uncle's hand and scuttled off. My uncle put his hand to his lips, sucked the wound a bit and said, "You were asleep and I saw a poisonous spider climbing down onto your neck from that branch. I put my hand out and it stung me."

Not a word did I believe; at least three times he had made attempts on my life in ways like that. But that spider had certainly bitten his hand, and the hand was swelling.

"You're my nephew," said Medardo.

"Yes," I replied in slight surprise, for it was the first time he gave any sign of recognizing me.

"I recognized you at once," he said, then added, "Ah, spider! I only have one hand and you want to poison that! But better my hand than this child's neck."

I had never known my uncle to speak like that. The thought went through my mind that he was telling the truth and maybe had gone good all of a sudden, but I at once put it aside; lies and intrigue were a habit with him. Certainly he seemed much changed, with an expression that was no longer tense and cruel but languid and drawn, perhaps from fear and pain at the bite. But his clothes, dusty and oddly cut, were also different, and helped to give that impression. His black cloak was a bit tattered, with dry leaves and chestnut husks sticking to the ends; his suit too was not of the usual black velvet but of threadbare fustian, and the leg was no longer encased in a high leather boot but in a blue and white striped woollen stocking.

To show I was not curious about him I went to see if any eel had taken a bite at my line. There were no eels, but slipped over the hook was a golden ring with a diamond in it. I pulled it up and saw that the stone bore the Terralba crest.

The Viscount's eye was following me, and he said, "Don't be surprised. As I passed I saw an eel wriggling on the hook and felt so sorry for it I freed it; then thinking of the loss I'd caused the fisherman by my action, I decided to repay him with my ring, the last thing of value I possess."

I stood there open-mouthed with amazement.

Medardo went on. "I didn't know at the time that the fisherman was you. Then I found you asleep on the grass and my pleasure at seeing you quickly turned to alarm at that spider coming down on you. The rest you already know." And so saying he looked sadly at his swollen purple hand.

All this might have been just a series of cruel deceptions, but I thought how lovely a sudden conversion of his feelings would be, and the joy it would also bring Sebastiana and Pamela and all the people suffering from his cruelty.

"Uncle," I said to Medardo, "wait for me here. I'll rush off to nurse Sebastiana who knows all about herbs and get her to give me one to heal spiders' bites."

"Nurse Sebastiana . . ." said the Viscount, as he lay outstretched with his hand on his chest, "How is she nowadays?"

I did not trust him enough to tell that Sebastiana had not caught leprosy and all I said was, "Oh, so so. I'm off now," and away I ran, longing more than anything else to ask Sebastiana what she thought of these strange developments.

I found the nurse still in her shack. I was panting with running and impatience, and gave her rather a confused account, but the old woman was more interested in Medardo's bite than in his acts of goodness. "A red spider, d'you say? Yes, yes, I know just the right herb . . Once a woodsman had his arm swell up . . . He's gone good, you say? Oh well, he always was, in a way, if one knew how to take him . . . Now where did I put that herb? Just make a poultice with it . . .

Yes, Medardo's always been a scatterbrain, ever since he was a child . . . Ah here's the herb, I'd put a little bag of it in reserve . . . Yes, he always was; when he got hurt he'd come and sob to his nurse . . . Is it a deep bite?"

"His left hand is all swollen up," said I.

"Oh, oh, you silly boy . . ." laughed the nurse. "The left hand . . . Where's Master Medardo's left hand? He left it behind in Bohemia with those Turks, may the devil take them, he left it there, with the whole left half of his body . . ."

"Oh yes, of course," I exclaimed. "And yet . . . he was there, I was here, he had his hand turned round like this . . . How can that be?"

"Can't you tell left from right any more?" said the nurse. "And yet you learnt when you were five . . ."

I just couldn't make it out. Sebastiana must be right, but I remembered exactly the opposite.

"Well, take him this herb, like a good boy," said the nurse, and off I ran.

Panting hard, I reached the brook, but my uncle was no longer there. I looked around; he had vanished with that swollen, poisoned hand of his.

That evening I was wandering among the olives. And there he was, wrapped in his black mantle, standing on a bank leaning against a tree trunk. His back was turned and he was looking out over the sea. I felt fear coming over me again, and with an effort managed to say in a faint voice, "Uncle, here is the herb for the bite . . ."

The half face turned at once and contracted into a ferocious sneer.

"What herb, what bite?" he cried.

"The herb to heal . . ." I said. But the sweet expression of before had vanished, it must have been but a passing moment's; perhaps it was slowly returning now in a tense smile, but that was obviously put on.

"Ah yes . . . fine . . . Put it in the hollow of that tree trunk . . . I'll take it later then," he said.

I obeyed and put my hand in the hollow. It was a wasps' nest. They all flew at me. I began to run, followed by the swarm, and flung myself into the stream. By swimming underwater I managed to put the wasps off my track. Raising my head I heard the Viscount's grim laugh in the distance.

Another time too he managed to deceive me. But there were many things I did not understand, and I went to Dr. Trelawney to talk to him about them. In his sexton's hut, by the light of a lantern, the Englishman was crouched over a book of human anatomy, very rare for him.

"Doctor," I asked him, "have you ever heard of a man bitten by a red spider coming through unharmed?"

"A red spider, did you say?" The doctor started. "Who had another bite from a red spider?"

"My uncle the Viscount," I said. "And I'd brought him a herb from Sebastiana, and from being good, as it seemed before, he became bad again and refused my help."

"I have just tended the Viscount for a red spider's bite on his hand," said Trelawney.

"Tell me, doctor, did you find him good or bad?"

Then the doctor described to me what had happened.

After I left the Viscount sprawled on the grass with his swollen hand Dr. Trelawney had passed that way. He noticed the Viscount and, seized with fear as always, tried to hide among the trees. But Medardo had heard his footsteps and got up and called, "Who's there?"

The Englishman thought, "If he finds it's me hiding from him there's no knowing what he won't do," and ran off so as not to be recognized. But he stumbled and fell into a pool in the stream. Although he had spent his life on ships, Dr. Trelawney did not know how to swim, and was threshing about in the middle of the pool shouting for help. Then the Viscount said, "Wait for me," went on to the bank and got into the water, swung by his aching hand on an extended tree root, and stretched out until his foot could be seized by the doctor. Long and thin as he was, he acted as a rope for the doctor to reach the bank.

There they are, both safe and sound, with the doctor stuttering, "Oh oh, m'lord . . . thank you indeed, m'lord . . . How can I? . . ." and he sneezes right in the other's face, as he'd caught a cold.

"Good luck!" says Medardo. "But cover yourself, please," and he puts his cloak over the doctor's shoulders.

The doctor protests, more confused than ever. And the Viscount exclaims, "Keep it, it's yours."

Then Trelawney notices Medardo's swollen hand. "What bit you?"

"A red spider."

"Let me tend it, m'lord."

And he takes him to his sexton's hut, where he does up the hand with medicines and bandages. Meanwhile the Viscount chats away with him, all humanity and courtesy. They part with a promise to see each other soon and reinforce their friendship.

"Doctor!" I said after listening to his tale. "The Viscount whom you tended shortly afterwards went back to his cruel madness and roused a whole nest of wasps against me."

"Not the one I tended," said the doctor with a wink.

"What d'you mean, doctor?"

"I'll tell you later. Now not a word to anyone. And leave me to my studies, as there are difficult times ahead."

And Doctor Trelawney took no more notice of me; back he went to that unusual reading of a treatise on human anatomy. He must have had some plan or other in his head, and for all the following days remained reticent and absorbed.

Now news of Medardo's double nature began coming from various sources. Children lost in the

woods were approached to their terror by the half
man with a crutch who led them home by the hand
and gave them figs and flowers and sweets; poor
widows were helped across brooks by him; dogs bitten
by snakes were tended, mysterious gifts were found on
thresholds and windowsills of the poor, fruit trees
torn up by the wind were straightened and put back
into their sockets before their owners had put a nose
outside the door.

At the same time, though, appearances of the
Viscount half wrapped in his black cloak were also a
signal for dire events; children were kidnapped and
later found imprisoned in caves blocked by stones;
branches broke off and rocks rolled onto old women;
newly ripe pumpkins were slashed to pieces from wan-
ton malice.

For some time the Viscount's crossbow had been
used only against swallows and in such a way as not
to kill but only wound and stun them, but now they
were seen in the sky with legs bandaged and tied to
splints, or with wings stuck together or waxed. A whole
swarm of swallows so treated were prudently flying
about together, like convalescents from a bird hospital,
and there was an incredible rumor that Medardo was
their doctor.

Once a storm caught Pamela, together with her
goat and duck, in a wild and distant spot. She knew that
nearby was a cave, very small, a kind of hollow in the
rock, and she went towards it. Sticking out of it she
saw a tattered and patched boot. Inside was huddling
the half body wrapped in its black cloak. She was

just going to run away, but the Viscount had already seen her, came out under the pouring rain and said to her, "Come, girl, take refuge here."

"No, I'm not taking any refuge there," said Pamela, "as there's scarcely room for one and you want to squeeze up to me."

"Don't be alarmed," said the Viscount. "I will stay outside and you take ease in there, with your goat and your duck too."

"The goat and duck can get wet."

"They'll take refuge too, you'll see."

Pamela, who had heard tell of strange impulses of goodness by the Viscount, said to herself, "We'll just see," and crouched down inside the cave, tight against her goat and duck. The Viscount stood up in front and held his cloak there like a tent so that neither she nor goat nor duck got wet. Pamela looked at the hand holding the cloak, remained for a moment deep in thought, began looking at her own hands, compared them to each other, then burst into a roar of laughter.

"I'm glad to see you so jolly, girl," said the Viscount. "But why are you laughing, if I may ask?"

"I'm laughing because I've understood what is driving all my fellow villagers quite mad."

"What is that?"

"That you are in part good and in part bad. Now it's all obvious."

"Why's that?"

"Because I've realized that you are the other half. The Viscount living in the castle, the bad one, is one half. And you're the other, who was thought lost in the war but has now returned. And it's a good half."

"That's nice of you. Thank you."

"Oh, it's the truth, not a compliment."

Now this was Medardo's story, as Pamela heard it that evening. It was not true that the cannon ball had blown part of his body to bits; it had split him in two halves. One was found by the army stretcher bearers, the other remained buried under a pyramid of Christian and Turkish corpses and was not seen. Deep in the night through the battlefield passed two hermits, whether faithful to the true religion or necromancers is not certain. They, as happens to some in wars, had been reduced to living in the no man's land between battlefields, and maybe, according to some nowadays, were trying to embrace at the same time the Christian Trinity and the Allah of Mahomet. In their peculiar piety these hermits, on finding Medardo's halved body, had taken him to their den, and there, with balsams and unguents prepared by themselves, tended and saved him. As soon as his strength was reëstablished the wounded man bade farewell to his saviors and, supported on his crutch, moved for months and years throughout all the nations of Christendom in order to return to his castle, amazing people along the way by his acts of goodness.

After having told Pamela his story, the good half of the Viscount asked the shepherd girl to tell him hers. Pamela explained how the bad Medardo was laying siege to her and how she had fled from home and was now wandering in the woods. At Pamela's account the good Medardo was moved, his pity divided between the goat girl's persecuted virtue, the bad Medardo's hopeless desolation, and the solitude of Pamela's poor parents.

"As for them," said Pamela, "my parents are just a pair of old rogues. There's no point in your pitying them."

"Oh, but just think of them, Pamela, how sad they'll be in their old home at this hour, without anyone to look after them and work the fields and do out the stall."

"It can fall on their heads can the stall, for all I care!" said Pamela. "I'm beginning to realize that you're a bit too soft, and instead of attacking that other half of yours for all the swinish things he does, you seem almost to pity him as well."

"Of course I do! I know what it means to be half a man, and of course I pity him."

"But you're different; you're a bit daft too, but good."

Then the good Medardo said, "Oh, Pamela, that's the good thing about being halved. One understands the sorrow of every person and thing in the world at its own incompleteness. I was whole and did not understand, and moved about deaf and unfeeling amid the pain and sorrow all round us, in places where as a whole person one would least think to find it. It's not only me, Pamela, who am a split being, but you and everyone else too. Now I have a fellowship which I did not understand, did not know before, when whole, a fellowship with all the mutilated and incomplete things in the world. If you come with me, Pamela, you'll learn to suffer with everyone's ills, and tend your own by tending theirs."

"That all sounds very fine," said Pamela, "but I'm in a great pickle with that other part of you being in love with me and my not knowing what he wants to do with me."

My uncle let his cloak fall, as the storm was over

"I'm in love with you too, Pamela."

Pamela jumped out of the cave. "What fun! There's the sign of the whale in the sky and I've a new lover! This one's halved too, but has a good heart."

They were walking under branches still dripping, through paths all mud. The Viscount's half mouth was curved in a sweet, incomplete smile.

"Well, what shall we do?" said Pamela.

"I'd say you ought to go back to your parents, poor things, and help them a bit in their work."

"You go if you want to," said Pamela.

"I do indeed want to, my dear," exclaimed the Viscount.

"I'll stay here," said Pamela, and stopped with her duck and goat.

"Doing good together is the only way to love."

"A pity. I thought there were other ways."

"Good-bye, my dear. I'll bring you some honey cake." And he hopped off on his stick along the path

"What d'you say, goatee? What d'you say, duck ling dear?" exclaimed Pamela when alone with her pets. "Why must all these oddities happen to *me?*"

{ 8 }

WHEN the news got around that the Viscount's other half had reappeared, things at Terralba became very different.

In the morning I accompanied Dr. Trelawney on his round of visits to the sick; for the doctor was gradually returning to the practice of medicine and was realizing how many ills our people suffered, their fibre undermined by the long famines of recent times —ills which he had not bothered about before.

We would go around the country lanes and find the signs of my uncle having preceded us. My good uncle, I mean, the one who every morning not only went the rounds of the sick, but also of the poor, the old, or whoever needed help.

In Bacciccia's orchard the ripe pomegranates were each tied round with a piece of rag. From this we understood that Bacciccia had a toothache. My uncle had wrapped up the pomegranates lest they fall off and be squashed, now that their owner's ills were preventing him from coming out and picking them himself;

but it was also a signal for Dr. Trelawney to pay the sick man a visit and bring his pincers.

Prior Cecco had a sunflower on his terrace in starved soil so that it never flowered. One morning we found three chickens tied on the railing there, all pecking grain as fast as they could and unloading their white excrement in the sunflower pot. We realized that the Prior must have diarrhoea. My uncle had tied up the chickens there to manure the sunflower, and also to warn Dr. Trelawney of this urgent case.

On old Giromina's steps we saw a row of snails moving up towards the door; they were big snails of the kind that are eaten cooked. This was a present from the woods brought by my uncle to Giromina, but also a sign that the old woman's heart disease had got worse and that the doctor should enter quietly lest he give her a fright.

All these methods of communication were used by the good Medardo so as not to alarm the sick by too brusque a request for the doctor's help, but also so that Trelawney should get some notion of the case to be treated before entering, and thus overcome his reluctance to set foot in the houses of others and to approach sick whose ills he did not know.

Suddenly throughout the valley ran the alarm, "The Bad 'Un! The Bad 'Un's coming."

It was my uncle's bad half who had been seen riding in the neighborhood. Then everyone ran to hide, Dr. Trelawney first, with me behind.

We passed by Giromina's, and on the steps was a streak of cracked snails, all slime and bits of shell.

"He's passed this way! Quick!"

On Prior Cecco's terrace the chickens were tied to the pan where tomatoes had been laid out to dry, and were ruining the lot.

"Quick!"

In Bacciccia's orchard the pomegranates had all been squashed on the ground and empty rag ends hung from the branches.

"Quick!"

So we spent out lives between doing good and being frightened. The Good 'Un (as my uncle's left half was called in contrast to the Bad 'Un who was the other) was now considered a saint. The maimed, the poor, the women betrayed, all those with troubles went to him. He could have profited by this to become Viscount himself. Instead of which he went on being a vagabond, going round half wrapped in his ragged black cloak, leaning on his crutch, his blue and white stocking full of holes, doing good both to those who asked him and to those who thrust him harshly from their doors. No sheep that broke a leg in a ravine, no drunk drawing a knife in a tavern, no adulterous wife hurrying to her lover by night but found him appearing as if dropped from the sky, black and thin and sweetly smiling, to help and advise, to prevent violence and sin.

Pamela was still in the woods. She had made herself a swing between two pine trees, then another firmer one for the goat and a lighter one for the duck, and she spent the hours swinging herself to and fro with her pets. But at fixed times the Good 'Un would come hobbling through the pine trees, with a bundle tied to his shoulder. It held clothes to be washed and mended which he had gathered from lonely beggars, orphans and sick; and he got Pamela to wash them, thus giving her a chance to do good too. Pamela, who was getting bored with always being in the woods, washed the clothes in the brook and he helped her. Then she hung them all to dry on the ropes of her swings, while the Good 'Un sat on a stone and read Tasso's "Jerusalem Liberated."

Pamela took no notice of the reading and lay on the grass taking it easy, delousing herself (for while living in the woods she had got a few on her), scratching herself with a plant whose literal name was "bum scratch," yawning, dangling stones in her bare toes, and looking at her legs, which were pink and plump as ever. The Good 'Un, without ever raising his eyes from the book, would go on declaiming octave after octave, with the aim of civilizing the rustic girl's manners.

But she, unable to follow the thread, and bored, was quietly inciting the goat to lick the Good 'Un's half face and the duck to perch on the book. The Good 'Un started back and raised the book, which closed. At that very moment the Bad 'Un appeared at a gallop among the trees, brandishing a great scythe against the Good 'Un. The scythe's blade fell on the book and cut it neatly in half lengthways. The back part remained in the Good 'Un's hand, and the rest fluttered through the air in a thousand half pages. The Bad 'Un vanished at a gallop; he had çertainly tried to scythe the Good 'Un's half-head off, but the goat and duck had appeared just at the right moment. Pages of Tasso with their white margins and halved verses flew about in the wind and came to rest on pine branches, on grass, on water in the brook. From the top of a hillock Pamela looked at the white flutter and cried, "How lovely!"

A few leaves reached a path along which Dr. Trelawney and I were passing. The doctor caught one in the air, turned it over and over, tried to decipher those verses with no head or tail to them and shook his head. "But I can't understand a thing . . . tst . . . tst . . ."

The Good 'Un's reputation even reached the Huguenots, and old Ezekiel was often seen standing on the highest terrace of yellow vineyard, gazing at the stony mule path up from the valley.

"Father," one of his sons said to him, "I see you are looking down into the valley as if awaiting someone's arrival."

" 'Tis man's lot to wait," replied Ezekiel, "and the just man's to wait with trust, the unjust man's with fear."

"Is it the Lame-One-on-the-other-foot that you are waiting for?"

"Have you heard him spoken of?"

"There's nothing else but the Half Man spoken of down in the valley. Do you think he will come up to us here?"

"If ours is the land of those who live in the right, and he is one who lives in the right, there is no reason why he should not come."

"The mule path is steep for one who has to do it on a crutch."

"There was a one-footed man who found himself a horse with which to come up."

Hearing Ezekiel talk, the other Huguenots had appeared from among the vines and gathered around him. And hearing an allusion to the Viscount they quivered silently.

"Father Ezekiel," they said, "that night when the Thin One came and the lightning burnt half the oak tree, you said that maybe one day we would be visited by a better traveller."

Ezekiel nodded and lowered his beard to his chest.

"Father, the one talked of now is as much a cripple as the other, his opposite in both body and soul, kind as the other was cruel. Could he be the visitor whom your words announced?"

"It could be every traveller on every road," said Ezekiel, "and so he, too."

"Then let's all hope that it be he!" said the Huguenots.

Ezekiel's wife came forward with her eyes fixed before her, pushing a wheelbarrow full of vine twigs.

"We always hope for everything good," said she, "but even if he who hobbles over these hills is but some poor soldier mutilated in the war, good or bad in soul, we must continue every day to do right and to cultivate our land."

"That is understood," replied the Huguenots. "Have we indeed said anything that meant the contrary?"

"Then, if we are all agreed," said the woman, "we can go back to our hoes and pitchforks."

"Plague and famine!" burst out Ezekiel. "Who told you to stop work, anyway?"

The Huguenots scattered among the vine rows to reach their tools left in the furrows, but at that moment Esau, who since his father was not looking had climbed up the fig tree to eat the early fruit, cried, "Down there! Who's arriving on that mule?"

A mule was in fact coming up the slope with half a man tied to the crupper. It was the Good 'Un, who had bought an old nag when they were just about to drown her in the stream as she was so far gone it was not worth sending her to the slaughterhouse.

"Anyway I'm only half a man's weight," he said to himself, "and the old mule might still bear me. And with my own mount I can go further and do more good." So his first journey was up to pay a visit to the Huguenots.

The Huguenots greeted him all lined up, standing stiffly to attention, singing a psalm. Then the old man went up to him and greeted him like a brother. The Good 'Un dismounted and answered these greetings ceremoniously, kissed the hand of Ezekiel's wife as she stood there grim and frowning, asked after everyone's health, put out his hand to stroke the tousled head of Esau, who drew back, interested himself in everyone's trouble, made them tell the story of their persecutions and was touched. They talked, of course, without dwelling on religious controversy, as if it were a sequence of misfortunes imputable to the general wickedness of man. Medardo passed over the fact that the persecutions were by the Church to which he belonged, and the Huguenots on their part did not launch out on any affirmations of faith, partly also for fear of saying things that were theologically mistaken. So they ended up by making vague charitable speeches, disapproving of all violence and excess. All were agreed, but it was a bit chilling on the whole.

Then the Good 'Un visited the fields, commiserated with them on the bad crops, and was pleased to hear that if nothing else they had a good crop of rye.

"How much d'you sell it for?" he asked.

"Three *scudi* the pound," said Ezekiel.

"Three *scudi* the pound? But the poor of Terralba are dying of hunger, my friends, and cannot buy even a handful of rye! Perhaps you don't know that hail has destroyed the rye crop in the valley, and you are the only ones who can preserve many families from famine?"

"We do know that," said Ezekiel. "And this is just why we can sell our rye well . . ."

"But think of the help it would be for those poor

people if you lowered the price . . . Think of the good you can do . . ."

Old Ezekiel stopped in front of the Good 'Un with arms crossed, and all the Huguenots imitated him.

"To do good, brother," he said, "does not mean lowering our prices."

The Good 'Un went over the fields and saw aged Huguenots like skeletons working the soil in the sun.

"You have a bad color," he said to an old man who had such a long beard he was hoeing it into the ground. "Don't you feel well?"

"Well as someone can feel who hoes for ten hours a day at the age of seventy with only thin soup in his belly."

"'Tis my cousin Adam," said Ezekiel, "an exceptional worker."

"At your age you must rest and nourish yourself," the Good 'Un was just saying, but Ezekiel dragged him brusquely away.

"All of us here earn our bread the hard way, brother," said he in a tone that admitted of no reply.

When he first got off his mule the Good 'Un had insisted on tying it up himself, and asked for a sack of fodder to refresh it after the climb. Ezekiel and his wife had looked at each other, as according to them a mule like that needed only a handful of wild chicory, but it was at the warmest moment of greeting the guest, and they had the fodder brought. Now though, thinking it over, old Ezekiel felt he really could not let that old carcass of a mule eat up the little fodder they had, and out of his guest's earshot he called Esau and said, "Esau, go quietly up to the mule, take the fodder away, and give it something else."

"A decoction for asthma?"

"Maize husks, chick-pea covers, what you like."

Off went Esau, took the sack from the mule and got a kick which made him walk lame for a time. To make up for this he hid the remaining fodder to sell on his own account, and said that the mule had finished the lot.

It was dusk. The Good 'Un was in the middle of the fields with the Huguenots and they no longer knew what to say to each other.

"We still have a good hour of work ahead of us, guest," said Ezekiel's wife.

"Well then, I'll leave you."

"Good luck to you, guest."

And back the good Medardo went on his mule.

"A poor creature, mutilated in the wars," said the woman when he had gone. "What a number there are round here! Poor wretches!"

"Poor wretches indeed," agreed the whole family.

"Plague and famine!" old Ezekiel was shouting as he went over the fields, fists raised at botched work and damage from drought. "Plague and famine!"

{ 9 }

OFTEN in the mornings I used to go to Pietrochiodo's workshop to see the ingenious carpenter's
constructions. He lived in growing anguish and re-
morse, since the Good 'Un had been visiting him at
night, reproving him for the tragic purpose of his
inventions, and inciting him to produce mechanisms
set in motion by good men and not by an evil urge
to torture.

"What machine should I make then, Master
Medardo?" asked Pietrochiodo.

"I'll tell you. For example you can . . ." and the
Good 'Un began to describe a machine which he
would have ordered were he the Viscount instead of
his other half, and to help out his explanation he traced
some confused designs.

Pietrochiodo thought at first that this machine
must be an organ, a huge organ whose keys would
produce sweet music, and was about to look for suitable wood for the pipes when from another conversa-
tion with the Good 'Un he got his ideas more con-

fused, as it seemed that Medardo wanted not air but wheat to pass through the pipes! In fact it was to be not only an organ but a mill grinding corn for the poor, and also possibly an oven for baking. Every day the Good 'Un improved his idea and covered more and more paper with plans, but Pietrochiodo could not manage to keep up with him; for this organ-cum-mill-cum-bakery was also to draw up water from wells, so saving donkeys' work, and was to move about on wheels for serving different villages, while on holidays it was to hang suspended in the air with nets all round, catching butterflies.

The carpenter was beginning to doubt whether building good machines was not beyond human possibility when the only ones which could function really practically and exactly seemed to be gibbets and racks. In fact as soon as the Bad 'Un explained to Pietrochiodo an idea for a new mechanism, the carpenter found a way of doing it occurring to him immediately; and he would set to work and would find every detail coming out perfect and irreplaceable, and the instrument when finished a masterpiece of ingenious technique.

The torturing thought came to the carpenter, "Can it be in my soul, this evil which makes only my cruel machines work?" But he went on inventing other tortures with great zeal and ability.

One day I saw him working on a strange instrument of execution, with a white gibbet framed in a wall of black wood. and a rope, also white, running

through two holes in the wall at the exact place of
the noose.

"What is that machine, Master?" I asked him.

"A gibbet for hanging in profile," he said.

"Who have you built it for?"

"For one man who both condemns and is condemned. With half of his head he condemns himself
to capital punishment, and with the other half he
enters the noose and breathes his last. I want to arrange
it so one can't tell which is which."

I realized that the Bad 'Un, feeling the popular-
ity of his good half growing, had arranged to get rid
of him as soon as possible.

In fact he called his constables and said, "For
far too long a low vagabond has been infesting our
estates and sowing discord. By tomorrow the criminal
must be captured and brought here to die."

"Lordship, it will be done," said the constables,
and off they went. Being one-eyed, the Bad 'Un had
not noticed that when answering him they had winked
at each other.

For it should be told that a palace plot had been
hatching in those days and the constabulary were part
of it too. The aim was to imprison and suppress the
reigning half-Viscount and hand castle and title over
to the other half. The latter however knew nothing
of this. And that night he woke up in the hayloft
where he lived and found himself surrounded by
constables.

"Have no fear," said the head constable. "The
Viscount has sent us to murder you, but we are weary

of his cruel tyranny and have decided to murder him
and put you in his place."

"What do I hear? Has this been done? I ask you.
The Viscount, you have not already murdered him,
have you?"

"No, but we surely will in the course of the
morning."

"Thanks be to Heaven! No, do not stain yourself
with more blood, too much has been shed already.
What good could come of rule born of crime?"

"No matter, we'll lock him in the tower and not
bother any more about him."

"Do not raise your hands against him or anyone
else, I beg you! I too am pained by the Viscount's
arrogance; yet the only remedy is to give him a good
example, by showing ourselves kind and virtuous."

"Then we'll have to murder you, Signore."

"Ah no! I told you not to murder anyone."

"What can we do then? If we don't suppress the
Viscount we must obey him."

"Take this phial. It contains a few drops, the
last that remain to me, of the unguent with which the
Bohemian hermits healed me and which till now
has been most precious to me at a change of weather,
when my great scar hurts. Take it to the Viscount and
say merely, "Here is a gift from one who knows
what it means to have veins that end in plugs!"

The constables took the phial to the Viscount,
who condemned them to be hanged. To save the
constables the other plotters planned a rising. They
were clumsy, and let out news of the revolt, which

was suppressed in blood. The Good 'Un took flowers
to the graves and consoled widows and orphans.

Old Sebastiana was never moved by the goodness
of the Good 'Un. When about his zealous enterprises,
the Good 'Un would often stop at the old nurse's
shack and visit her, always full of kindness and con-
sideration. And every time she would preach him a
sermon. Perhaps because of her maternal instinct,
perhaps because old age was beginning to cloud her
mind, the nurse took little account of Medardo's
separation into two halves. She would criticize one
half for the misdeeds of the other, give one advice
which only the other could follow and so on.

"Why did you cut off the head of old Granny
Bigin's chicken, poor old woman, which was all she
had? You're too grown-up now to do such things . . ."

"Why d'you say that to me, nurse? You know it
wasn't me . . ."

"Oho! Then just tell me who it was?"

"Me but—"

"There, you see!"

"But not me here . . ."

'Ah, because I'm old you think I'm soft too, do
you? When I hear people talk of some rascality I can
tell at once if it's one of yours. And I say to myself, I
swear Medardo's hand is in that . . ."

"But you're always mistaken . . ."

'I'm mistaken, am I! You young people tell us old folk that we're mistaken . . . And what about you? You went and gave your crutch to old Isodoro . . ."

"Yes, that was me. . . ."

"D'you boast of it? He used it for beating his wife, poor woman . . ."

"He told me he couldn't walk because of gout . . ."

"He was pretending . . . And you at once go and give him your crutch . . . Now he's broken it on his wife's back and you go round on a twisted branch . . . You've no head, that's what's the matter with you! Always like this! And what about that time when you made Bernardo's bull drunk with *grappa* . . ."

"That wasn't . . ."

"Oho, so it wasn't you! That's what everyone says, but it's always him, the Viscount!"

The Good 'Un's frequent visits to Pratofungo were due, apart from his filial attachment to the nurse, to the fact that he was then dedicating himself to helping the poor lepers. Immune from contagion (also due, apparently to the mysterious cures of the hermits) he would wander about the village informing himself minutely of each one's needs, and not leave them in peace until he had done every conceivable thing he could for them. Often he would go to and fro on his mule between Pratofungo and Dr. Trelawney's, for advice and medicines. The doctor himself had not the courage to go near the lepers, but he seemed, with

the good Medardo as intermediary, to be beginning
to take an interest in them.

But my uncle's intentions went further. He was
proposing to tend not only the bodies of the lepers
but their souls too. And he was forever among them,
moralizing away, putting his nose into their affairs,
being scandalized, and preaching. The lepers could
not endure him. Pratofungo's happy licentious days
were over. With this thin figure on his one leg, black-
dressed, ceremonious and sententious, no one could
have fun without arousing public recriminations,
malice and backbiting. Even their music, by dint of
being criticized as futile, lascivious and inspired by evil
sentiments, grew burdensome and those strange instruments of theirs got covered with dust. The leper
women, deprived of their revels, suddenly found themselves face to face with their disease and spent their
evenings sobbing in despair.

"Of the two halves the Good 'Un is worse than
the Bad 'Un," they began to say at Pratofungo.

But it was not only among the lepers that
admiration for the Good 'Un was decreasing.

"Lucky that cannon ball only split him in two,"
everyone was saying. "If it had done it in three, who
knows what we'd have to put up with!"

The Huguenots now kept guard in turns to
protect themselves from him too, as he had now lost
respect for them, and would come up at all hours

spying out how many sacks were in their granaries, and preaching to them about their prices being too high and spreading this around, so ruining their business.

Thus the days went by at Terralba, and our sensibilities became numbed, since we felt ourselves lost between an evil and a virtue equally inhuman.

{ 10 }

THERE is never a moonlight night but wicked ideas in evil souls writhe like serpents in nests, and charitable ones sprout lilies of renunciation and dedication. So Medardo's two halves wandered, tormented by opposing furies, amid the crags of Terralba.

Then each came to a decision on his own, and next morning set out to put it into practice.

Pamela's mother was just about to draw water when she stumbled into a snare and fell into the well. She hung on a rope and shrieked "Help!" Then, in the circle of the wellhead, against the sky she saw the silhouette of the Bad 'Un, who said to her, "I just wanted to talk to you. This is what I've decided. Your daughter Pamela is often seen about with a halved vagabond. You must make him marry her. He has compromised her now and if he's a gentleman he must put it right. That's my decision: don't ask me to explain more."

Pamela's father was taking a sack of olives from his grove to the oil press, but the sack had a hole in it, and a dribble of olives followed him along the path. Feeling his burden grown lighter, the old man took the sack from his shoulders and realized it was almost empty. But behind him he saw the Good 'Un gathering up the olives one by one and putting them in his cloak.

"I was following you in order to have a word and had the good fortune of saving your olives. This is what is in my heart. For some time I have been thinking that the unhappiness of others which I desire to help is perhaps increased by my very presence. I intend to leave Terralba. But I do so only if my departure will give peace back to two people—to your daughter who sleeps in a cave while a noble destiny awaits her, to my unhappy right part who should not be left so lonely. Pamela and the Viscount must be united in matrimony."

Pamela was training a squirrel when she met her mother, who was pretending to look for pine cones.

"Pamela," said her mother, "the time has come for that vagabond called the Good 'Un to marry you."

"Where does that idea come from?" said Pamela.

"He has compromised you and he shall marry you. He's so kind that if you tell him so he won't say no."

"But how did you get such an idea in your head?"

"Quiet! If you knew who told me you wouldn't ask so many questions; it was the Bad 'Un in person told me, our most illustrious Viscount!"

"Oh dear!" said Pamela, dropping the squirrel in her lap. "I wonder what trap he's preparing for us."

Soon afterwards she was teaching herself to hum

through a blade of grass when she met her father, who was pretending to look for wood.

"Pamela," said her father, "it's time you said 'yes' to the Viscount, the Bad 'Un, on condition you marry in church."

"Is that your idea or someone else's?"

"Wouldn't you like to be a Viscountess?"

"Answer my question."

"All right; imagine, it was told me by the best-hearted man in all the world, the vagabond they call the Good 'Un."

"Oh, that one has nothing else to think of. You wait and see what I arrange!"

Ambling through the thickets on his gaunt horse, the Bad 'Un thought over his stratagem; if Pamela married the Good 'Un then by law she would be wife to Medardo of Terralba, his wife that is. By this right the Bad 'Un would easily be able to take her from his rival, so meek and unaggressive.

Then he met Pamela, who said to him, "Viscount, I have decided that we'll marry if you are willing."

"You and who?" exclaimed the Viscount.

"Me and you, and I'll come to the castle and be the Viscountess."

The Bad 'Un had not expected this at all, and thought, "Then it's useless to arrange all the play-

acting of getting her married to my other half; I'll
marry her myself and that'll be that."

So he said, "Right."

Pamela said, "Arrange things with my father."

A little later Pamela met the Good 'Un on his
mule.

"Medardo," she said, "I realize now that I'm
really in love with you and if you wish to make me
happy you must ask for my hand in marriage."

The poor man, who had made that great renunciation for love of her, sat open-mouthed. "If she's
happy to marry me, I can't get her to marry the other
one any more," he thought, and said, "My dear, I'll
hurry off to see about the ceremony."

"Arrange things with my mother, do," said she.

All Terralba was in a ferment when it was known
that Pamela was to marry. Some said she was marry-
ing one, some the other. Her parents seemed to be
trying to confuse ideas on purpose. Up at the castle
everything was certainly being polished and decorated
for a great occasion. And the Viscount had made a
suit of black velvet with a big puff on the sleeve and
another on the thigh. But the vagabond had also had
his poor mule brushed up and mended his clothes at

elbow and knee. In church all the candelabras were aglitter.

Pamela said that she would not leave the wood until the moment of the nuptial procession. I did the commissions for her trousseau. She sewed herself a white dress with a veil and a long train and made up a circlet and belt of lavender sprigs. As she still had a few yards of veil left, she made a wedding robe for the goat and a wedding dress for the duck, and so ran through the woods, followed by her two pets, until the veil got all torn in the branches and her train gathered every pine cone and chestnut husk drying along the paths.

But the night before the wedding she was thoughtful and a bit alarmed. Sitting at the top of a hillock bare of trees, with her train wrapped round her feet, her lavender circlet all awry, she propped her chin on her hand and looked round sighing at the woods.

I was always with her, for I was to act as page, together with Esau, who was, however, not to be found.

"Who will you marry, Pamela?" I asked her.

"I don't know," she said. "I really don't know what might happen. Will it go well? Will it go badly?"

Every now and again from the woods rose a kind of guttural cry or a sigh. It was the two halved swains who, prey to the excitement of the vigil were wandering through glades in the woods, wrapped in their black cloaks, one on his bony horse, the other on his bald mule, moaning and sighing in anxious imaginings. And the horse leaped over ledges and landslides, and the mule clambered over slopes and hillsides, without their two riders ever meeting.

Then at dawn the horse, urged to a gallop, was lamed in a ravine; and the Bad 'Un could not get to the wedding in time. The mule on the other hand went slowly and carefully and the Good 'Un reached the church punctually, just as the bride arrived with her train held by me and by Esau, who had finally been dragged down.

The crowd was a bit disappointed at seeing that the only bridegroom to arrive was the Good 'Un leaning on his crutch. But the marriage was duly celebrated, the bride and groom said yes and the ring was passed and the priest said, "Medardo of Terralba and Pamela Marcolfi, I hereby join you in holy matrimony."

Just then from the end of the nave, supporting himself on his crutch, entered the Viscount, his new velvet suit slashed, dripping and torn. And he said, "I am Medardo of Terralba and Pamela is my wife."

The Good 'Un staggered up face to face with him. "I am the Medardo whom Pamela has married."

The Bad 'Un flung away his crutch and put his hand to his sword. The Good 'Un had no option but do the same.

"On guard!"

The Bad 'Un threw himself into a lunge, the Good 'Un went into defense, but both of them were soon rolling on the floor.

They agreed that it was impossible to fight bal-

anced on one leg. The duel must be put off to be
better prepared.

"D'you know what I'll do?" said Pamela. "I'm
going back to the woods." And away she ran from
the church, with no pages any longer holding her
train. On the bridge she found the goat and duck
waiting, and they trotted along beside her.

The duel was fixed for dawn next day in the
Nun's Field. Master Pietrochiodo invented a kind
of leg in the shape of a compass which, fixed to the
halved men's belts, would allow them to stand upright and move and even bend their bodies backwards
and forwards, while the point kept firmly in the
ground. Galateo the leper, who had been a gentleman when in health, acted as umpire; the Bad 'Un's
seconds were Pamela's father and the chief constable,
the Good 'Un's, two Huguenots. Dr. Trelawney stood
by to lend his services, and arrived with a huge roll
of bandages and a demijohn of balsam, as if to tend a
battlefield. A lucky thing for me since he needed my
help to carry all those things.

It was a greenish dawn; on the field the two
thin black duelists stood still with swords at the
ready. The leper blew his horn; it was the signal; the
sky quivered like taut tissue; dormice in their lairs
dug claws into soil, magpies with heads under wings
tore feathers from their sides and hurt themselves,
worms' mouths ate their own tails, snakes bit them-

selves with their own teeth, wasps broke their stings on stones, and everything turned against itself. Frost lay in wells, lichen turned to stone and stone to lichen, dry leaves to mould, and trees were filled by thick hard sap. So man moved against himself, both hands armed with swords.

Once again Pietrochiodo had done a masterly job. The compass legs made circles on the field and the duelers flung themselves into assaults of clanking metal and thudding wood, into feints and lunges. But they did not touch each other. At every lunge the sword's point seemed to go straight at the adversary's fluttering cloak, and each seemed determined to make for the part where there was nothing, that is the part where he should have been himself. Certainly if instead of half duelers there had been two whole ones, they would have wounded each other again and again. The Bad 'Un fought with fury and ferocity, yet never managed to launch his attacks just where his enemy was; the Good 'Un had correct mastery, but never did more than pierce the Viscount's cloak.

At a certain point they found themselves sword-guard to sword-guard; the points of their wooden legs were stuck in the ground like stakes. The Bad 'Un freed himself with a start and was just losing his balance and rolling to the ground when he managed to give a terrific swing not right on his adversary but very close; a swing parallel to the margin interrupting the Good 'Un's body, and so near that it was not clear at once if it was this side or the other. But soon we saw the body under the cloak go purple with blood from head to groin and there was no more doubt. The Good 'Un swayed, but as he fell in a last wide, almost pitiful, movement he too swung his sword very near his rival, from head to abdomen, between the point where the Bad 'Un's body was not and the point where it might have been. Now the Bad 'Un's body also spouted blood along the whole length of the huge old wound; the lungs of both had burst all their vein ends and reopened the wound which had divided them in two. Now they lay face to face and the blood which had once been one man's alone again mingled in the field.

Aghast at this sight I had not noticed Trelawney; then I realized that the doctor was jumping up and down with joy on his grasshopper's legs, clapping his hands and shouting, "He's saved, he's saved! He's saved! Leave it to me."

Half and hour later we bore back one single wounded man on a stretcher to the castle. Bad and Good 'Uns had been tightly bound together; the doctor had taken great care to get all guts and arteries of both parts to correspond, and then a mile of bandages had tied them together so tightly that he looked more like an ancient embalmed corpse than a wounded man.

My uncle was watched night and day as he lay between life and death. One morning looking at that face crossed by a red line from forehead to chin and on down the neck, it was Sabastiana who first said, "There, he's moved."

A quiver was in fact going over my uncle's features, and the doctor wept for joy at seeing it transmitted from one cheek to the other.

Finally Medardo shut his eyes and his lips: at first his expression was lopsided; he had one eye frowning and the other supplicating, a forehead here corrugated and there serene, a mouth smiling in one corner and gritting its teeth in the other. Then gradually it became symmetrical again.

Dr. Trelawney said, "Now he's healed."

And Pamela exclaimed, "At last I'll have a husband with everything complete."

So my uncle Medardo became a whole man again, neither good nor bad, but a mixture of goodness and badness, that is, apparently not dissimilar to what he had been before the halving. But having had the experience of both halves each on its own, he was bound to be wise. He had a happy life, many children and a just rule. Our life too changed for the better. Some might expect that with the Viscount entire again, a period of marvellous happiness would open, but obviously a whole Viscount is not enough to make all the world whole.

Now Pietrochiodo built gibbets no longer, but mills, and Trelawney neglected his will-'o-the-wisps for measles and chickenpox. I, though, amid all this fervor of wholeness, felt myself growing sadder and more lacking. Sometimes one who thinks himself incomplete is merely young.

I had reached the threshold of adolescence and still hid among the roots of the great trees in the wood to tell myself stories. A pine needle could represent a knight, or a lady, or a jester. I made them move before my eyes and enraptured myself in interminable tales about them. Then I would be overcome with shame at these fantasies and would run off.

A day came when Dr. Trelawney left me too. One morning into our bay sailed a fleet of ships flying the British flag and anchored offshore. The whole of Terralba went to the seashore to look at them, except me, who did not know. The gunwales and rigging were full of sailors carrying pineapples and tortoises and waving scrolls with maxims on them in Latin and English. On the quarterdeck, amid officers in tricorn and wig, Captain Cook fixed the shore with his telescope, and as soon as he sighted Dr. Trelawney gave orders for him to be signalled by flag, "Come on board at once, Doctor, as we want to get on with that game of cards."

The doctor bade farewell to all at Terralba and left us. The sailors intoned an anthem, "Oh, Australia!" And the doctor was hitched on board astride a barrel of *cancarone*. Then the ships drew anchor.

I had seen nothing. I was deep in the wood telling myself stories. When I heard later, I began running towards the seashore crying, "Doctor! Doctor Trelawney! Take me with you! Doctor, you can't leave me here!"

But already the ships were vanishing over the horizon and I was left behind, in this world of ours full of responsibilties and will-'o-the-wisps.